Goodbye to Russia

Sammie Adetiloye

Published by New Generation Publishing in 2021

First Edition

ISBN 978-1-80369-200-5

www.newgeneration-publishing.com

New Generation Publishing

Sammie Adetiloye was born in southwest Nigeria in 1969. For some years he pursued a career in journalism in Hungary after obtaining a diploma in News-writing and Journalism from London School of Journalism. In 2008 he came to England to further his education. He obtained a BA (HONS) degree in English Language and Literature in 2016; a Master's degree in Creative Writing in 2018 from The Open University; and a Cambridge University Certificate in English Language Teaching to Adults in 2019 from South Thames College, London. His special interests are reading and writing short stories. He hopes you enjoy these collected short stories.

Contents

Preface

Most of the stories recorded in this collection really occurred. One or two were experiences of my own. The rest were those told to me by friends of mine. The events in *Goodbye to Russia* were experienced by me some years gone by. But, as the world has become a global village, the racial intolerance that brought about those kinds of incidents may no longer exist. However, the aim of the story is to open the eyes of Africans who journey across continents or the Mediterranean Sea in their quest for political or economic adventure to the need for precautions. *The African Boy* is drawn from life, common to African children who often quickly succumb to disease because of the poor hygienic conditions they live in. *The State of the Nation* is based on the experience of a frustrated young man who has lost confidence in the ability of his government to provide employment for its youths.

Although this collection of short stories is intended mainly to sensitise young African adventurers, I hope it will not be shunned by non-Africans on that account, for part of my plan has been to use some of the stories to speak to the conscience of foreign leaders who work collaboratively with African leaders, with criminal behaviour, who have nothing to offer their citizens other than a frightful spectacle of poverty and corruption. It gives me a feeling of inner apprehensive disquiet when I see that African leaders cannot provide their people with employment to keep them back home on the continent.

Putting the stories together has not been easy. Each story here has a beginning, middle and an end. The main challenge was how to find the appropriate language and refreshing expressions to make the stories as easy as possible to read, and to bring out their morals to you, the reader, regardless of your social and cultural background.

In truth, I could not have achieved my current level of success without a strong support of my wife, Funmi Adetiloye, who supported me with love and understanding. For this, I am deeply grateful.

Sammie Adetiloye

The African Boy

I can't consult my horoscope. The truth is that I don't know my exact age. My birth certificate is lost. My father didn't keep it. My mother doesn't have a clue about its whereabouts.

What I do know is that my younger brother, Anthony, was born in 1960. When I grew up to know the importance of the record of birth, I assumed that I'd be about two years older than Anthony. I decided to set my own date of birth to 1958, October 10. I've been going about my adult life with this invented declaration of age.

I'm John Iroko. I'm a product of a broken home. I know poverty very well. I was born into a polygamous family under the discipline of a strict and violent father, a cocoa farmer. I'm the fifth child of my father's six children. He had a girl by his first wife; a boy and two girls by his second; and me and Anthony by a woman who was my father's third and last wife, Elizabeth, a housewife. My father loved his other two wives and their children, but he hated me and my mother - the recipient of my father's violent behaviour. And why was my mother the target of my father's aggressive behaviour? You may want to find out. Well, my mother dropped me a hint.

I was raised in a small town called Uso in Nigeria. The town had no electricity. Everyone relied on candlelight, torch-lights and lanterns at night. Roads and streets were dirty and dusty in the dry season. It was common to find heaps of rubbish of yester years uncollected. In the rainy season, the roads were muddy and flooded which made them unsafe for children. When the weather was windy, the moan of the wind in the surrounding forest was like the distant singing of a group of sinners confessing their sins to God.

I lived with my parents in a large mud house with bamboos as beams and a corrugated iron roof. Each of my father's three wives had a room and a parlour to herself and her children. Dung of cows and goats was used for plastering the interior walls. On the outside, the walls had rough surface where thousands of cold-blooded lizards could be seen warming themselves in the early morning sunshine. By the evening they'd all go to sleep in the narrow gaps in the walls. To warm the house in the rainy season, we'd stoke fires in the middle of the rooms. Anthony and I usually sat opposite a bright fire, staring at the flames. Around the house, my father built a mud fence (ten feet tall) on which several thousand pieces of broken bottles were laid to deter intruders from climbing over it. And along the fence line, my father grew tobacco plants whose pungent aroma helped to keep snakes away.

It was in this house as I have described it to you that my father ruled his family with an iron fist and kept his wives like rusty coins which can't be put into circulation.

But in our district, my father came across as a wise man. Sometimes in the afternoon when he was not on the farm and the weather was clement, my father would sit in the shade of a leafy mango tree in front of our neighbour's house and listen to world news in the local language on his World Receiver transistor radio. To give my father his due, you could count on your fingers the number of men in the town who listened to national and international news as my father did. It's not at all surprising that young people, for their own benefit, would sit with him under the tree to get the lowdown on the latest national and international affairs. Some would pour out their troubles to my father for his advice.

I started primary school at the age of six. Time has left a gap in my memory about what actually happened on my first day at school. But I remember that in order to determine if I was ripe (age-wise) to start school, I was taken before the headmaster of the only primary school in the town. He asked me to stand erect, head straight, and to stretch my right hand over my head to touch my left ear. And having successfully carried out the exercise, I was offered a seat in a classroom of about twenty pupils.

Life was very hard for me in my childhood. It was hard to find food to feed my hungry month. Hunger and the fear of my father's violent behaviour interfered with my ability to concentrate at school, as time went by. Sometimes, I sat down listlessly on the school premises, or walked in circles, trying to search the glass cell of my memory for a particular incident which would suddenly recall to me the moment when I had shared a laugh with my father.

One afternoon my father's violent behaviour towards my mother laid itself out before me like a map. I'd just come back home from school when I saw my parents arguing. I can't remember the offensive comment which my father had accused my mother of making about one of his other two wives.

That afternoon my mother was sitting on a straw mat on the verandah. She was blowing the chaff off the local rice on a tray she balanced on her knees. She appeared not to be paying too much of attention to a torrent of abuse my father was letting out.

You see, it is generally thought that a woman will get the better of a man where the tongue is concerned, but my father was in a class of his own. But now and then my mother answered back to my father, not allowing him to have the last word.

'Hey, don't open that your dirty mouth again to answer me back!' my father boomed like a bass viol.

And in less time than it takes the ash to fall off a cigarette, my father's eyes had turned red and bulged out like those of a toad. Fear knotted my stomach, as I watched my father moving aggressively towards my mother. He grabbed my mother, brought her to her full height, and pinned her against the rough surface of the mud wall. My mother's head soon bent under the rain of blows that descended on her head. She gave a gasp and burst into a flood of tears.

'Kill me today, once and for all,' my mother said amid sobs.

My younger brother, Anthony, crying hysterically, squeezed himself in between his parents in an effort to pull my father away, but he was unsuccessful. Quick as a flash, I ran to my father and sank my teeth into his bum. He let out a sharp cry of his own before unlocking his grip on my mother's neck. In retaliation, my father gave me a backhand slap which sent me crashing into a bucket of water kept nearby. My mother, now being able to break free from my father's grip, ran into her room and slammed the door shut. My father gave the door a few kicks while he was looking over his shoulder, as he was not sure of what physical harm I could do to him with his back turned to me.

On that day in the middle of the night, I was awoken by my mother's muffled gasping, as though she were choking. I quickly lit a candle and took some water with me to sprinkle on her in case she should faint. I saw my mother sitting on the edge of her cane bed, struggling to keep down her sobs. I patted my mother's shoulder and encouraged her to sleep.

'Bring me that hand mirror,' she said.

My mother looked at her face in the mirror with the candlelight.

'Look at my face,' my mother said between sobs. 'Look at what your father has done to me!'

Looking at my mother's swollen face, I felt like I should kill my father that night for my mother to have peace.

Three days later when my father was on the farm with his other wives, my mother, who had been weeping like the lost since my father beat her like a drum, took all her movable belongings and left home. She took my ten-year-old brother, Anthony, with her. But a day before my mother left, she had gathered me and Anthony together as a hen gathers her brood under her wings. She warned me in a low tone to avoid getting into trouble with my father. I didn't know what she intended to do. But she said enough was enough.

'Mum,' I said. 'Why does my father hate you this much?'

'He had once told me he was not your father.'

'And is it true?'

My mother said she had never been unfaithful to my father. And I believe her. Those who know me and knew my father very well see me as a spitting image of the man. Only God can take responsibility for that. But my father couldn't see himself in me or me in him. Sad!

The day my mother left I was at school. When I arrived home, the door of my mother's room was open. I shouted my usual afternoon greetings, thinking that my mother was inside, but there was no response. I entered the room and realized that my mother's clothes on the racks had disappeared. I was running around in the room like a dog chasing its tail. I came out to see if the clothes had been washed and hung out to dry. The clothes lines were empty. I went back in and I realized that her sandals and flip-flops behind the door had also disappeared. I sat down on the floor. I bent my head down to my lap in front of my mother's empty room, with tears running down my cheeks.

Now, the sun was dying, round and yellow as a pumpkin when my father and his other two wives arrived home from the farm. My father saw me first. I was still in my school uniform, stained with tears.

'Why are you crying?'

'I can't find my mother.'

My father put down his cutlass and went into my mother's room. He came out and grabbed my shoulders and shook me violently.

'Where, where's your mother?' he asked.

'I don't know,' I said.

My father left me hurriedly and went back into my mother's room as if he was not sure of what he had seen at first. His other two wives joined him to inspect the empty room. When he came out again I had kept a safe distance. He swore and cursed in helpless fury as sweat trickled over his cracked lips. He put his right index finger on his lips and was staring into space. On that day, not a morsel of food crossed my lips. A day lapsed into a week, a week into a month, and no news came about my mother's whereabouts.

The departure and the perceived infidelity of my mother worsened the relationship between me and my father. My father began to use me like a slave. If I made any small mistakes, he would abuse me in the severest possible tone. At home, I always felt I was a soul apart, cut off from normal human happiness. He would not let me sleep in my mother's room. He moved me into a small room like a pantry where he had kept his old Raleigh bicycle. The room had a door which couldn't close because its hinges had broken. So it was difficult to fence off mosquitoes. One morning, I woke up and saw scores of mosquitoes on the wall. Their abdomens were full of blood. Most of them were now lazy and unable to fly when I touched them.

My father never hesitated to put me in harm's way. He would send me out on errands when the rain was pounding the roof and the town was flooded, or when a howling wind was playing the surrounding trees like a flute. I remember one night when this kind of weather prompted my younger brother, Anthony, to ask my mother: 'Mama, who is playing music behind the house?'

Mostly on an empty stomach, I'd keep the surroundings of our house free from weeds. At weekends, I'd carry piles of dirty laundry belonging to my father and his other wives to the river to wash. Then I'd spread the clothes on the grass and watch them dry before coming home. If it was a day the sun was blazing in the sky like a disc of an electric cooker, I'd sit down at the river bank to cool off and watch birds bob their tails, clear their throats and sing cheerfully in the trees.

Now at the age of twelve, I decided to shift for myself. I completely withdrew the unquestioning obedience which my father thought I owed to him. I stopped being used like a slave in the house. My father began to see me as a boy rapidly growing as wild as a weed.

Every working day, I'd go to the quarry on the outskirts of the town to break rocks into cobblestones with a huge hammer I could hardly carry. I'd come back home with open wounds in my legs; a face caked with dust, and grit in the eyes. At weekends when the site was closed, I'd go about the town with my big head on a thin neck and begged party-organizers to give me a few odds and ends. On several occasions I received knocks on the head for daring to come near V.I.P tables with a cloud of flies following me about because of a foul lingering smell from the festering wounds in my legs.

In the absence of my brother, Anthony, the only friend I had at the time was a strange old female cat. I believe she must have seen that I was alone and lonely. The cat would visit me in the evening when I came back from the quarry. First, she'd sit on the fence and say 'meow, meow'. After that she'd climb down, tail up, and swagger towards me in the room. She then purred and rubbed her face against my legs. If I was sitting on a stool, she jumped onto my lap and allowed me to stroke her. One evening, she visited me carrying a dead mouse. She dropped her kill at my feet. The mouth and the whiskers of the cat were stained with blood. I carried her in the crook of my arm and stroked her, not minding the stains in her mouth. 'Thank you,' I said, 'but I can't share this food with you.'

Sadly, I lost this friend when my father sent me out of the house. A plea to my father from his family to allow me to come back home was rejected. I can't remember what he said my offence was. But I strongly felt that he had thought that my mother owed him a debt which I had to pay, with interest. I began to sleep rough. One day in the open, another day in the market place until I finally moved to an abandoned ramshackle house near the quarry site and took a room there. It was in this house I'd cook my cocoyam with nothing but a pinch of salt to jack up the flavor on my tongue.

When my father died of cancer at the age of fifty-two, I'd already lived on the street for more than three hundred and sixty-five days of the year. Those who knew him in town thought he'd died at a time when he was still as strong as an oak tree, but I didn't feel slightly sorry for his early death.

After my father's death, I came back home to pick up the pieces of my life. I was reunited with my brother, Anthony, and my mother who came back from self-exile to grieve over her husband's death, as tradition demanded. Now at fourteen, I went back to school to complete my primary and secondary education. Today, I hold a Master's degree in journalism. But when I look back at my nervous childhood days, how my own father had disturbed the tenor of my life, and the fact that I still can't consult my horoscope, anger still flames up in my heart.

A Crying Shame

It is not unusual to find people sleeping rough on the streets. But nobody could bring themselves to imagine that a retired qualified nurse midwife should be the occupant of a house of carton boxes and plastic sheeting near a heap of rubbish on a busy street in Lagos.

Alice Gooder was a sixty-eight-year-old widow. She was tall, thin, with a face as black as shoe polish. Her skin, crawled over by flies, had withered like flowers languishing from a lack of fresh air and water. Alice was dressed in a pair of dirty jean trousers and a sleeveless top. Every afternoon Alice would sit in front of her house of carton, with hands outstretched in an appeal for alms.

Six months earlier, Alice had had trouble with her landlord over an accumulated debt of unpaid rents. The day she was given a notice to quit, the landlord thought he had had enough. Gritting her teeth in silent fury, Alice went to the bank where she drew her monthly pension to have words with the bank manager.

When Alice entered the bank, a young lady came out of the manager's office to attend to her.

'This is the third time I've come here in the last one month. What's going on with my pension?'

'Please, take a seat. What's your name, madam?' the young lady said.

'Mrs Alice Gooder.'

The young clerk went into another office apparently looking for Alice's file. After spending about fifteen minutes, she came out, mopping the sweat that was now glistering on her forehead with the sleeve of her uniform.

'Sorry, madam,' the clerk said. 'Your pension provider has relocated to the Federal Capital, Abuja. We no longer have your fund paid to us.'

'What!'

For a moment Alice was silent. Then she gave a gasp of anger. Her fingers twisted into claws, and the young clerk watched helplessly, as two tears trickled down Alice's nose. She went back home. In a low monotone, Alice addressed her reflection in the mirror exactly as though she were talking to another person.

'O God, when shall I fall on my bended knees and thank God I'm a citizen of this country?'

Later in the day Alice sent a message to her daughter (her only child), Patricia, who was living with her husband, Julius, in Benin City. Alice had asked her daughter for financial help. But when no reply was forthcoming after thirty days, and the end of her two-week quit notice was near, Alice sold all her saleable belongings, and paid off her rent arrears. She had thought that after settling her bills she would continue to live in the apartment even though it was now empty of furniture, but the landlord refused. Alice put her toilet things, a night dress and a change of clothes into a plastic bag and travelled to Benin City with the hope of staying with her daughter and son-in-law until such a time when she would be able to sort out the problem with her pension.

When Alice arrived in Benin City, it was a bitterly hot Friday afternoon. Her daughter and son-in-law had not come back home from work. She looked at her watch. It was half-three. Her daughter would probably arrive home at four. Alice sat on a bench under a mango tree in front of the house. While she was waiting, she saw a ripe mango hanging low from the tree. She plucked it and dug her teeth into the flesh. Alice was still noisily sucking out the mango juice, when Patricia and Julius arrived home together.

Patricia was thirty-two, a lively and chatty sort of person. Julius was a bit shy, but occasionally brash. He enjoyed the company of his wife for her jocose personality. Patricia and Julius were surprised but happy to see Alice in front of their house. Patricia ran to her mother and embraced her, while Julius watched with a bright smile on his face.

'Mum, you didn't send us a message before coming,' Patricia said.

'Sorry, my dear, for this unexpected visit,' Alice said.

'That's alright, ma,' Julius said. 'You're always welcome.'

'Thank you, Julius. I did send a message through post a month ago,' Alice said.

'We haven't received it yet, mum,' Patricia said.

Patricia held her mother's hand, as they went into the house – a three-bedroom two-storey house. Patricia quickly arranged the visitor's room downstairs for her mother to stay in. Later in the evening after dinner, Alice thanked Julius for welcoming her. Alice explained to her daughter and son-in-law how she had fallen on hard times after using up her savings in Lagos because of the non-payment of her pension.

'On Monday I'll travel to Abuja to see the pension officials, Alice said.'

When Alice met with the pension officer in Abuja, Alice complained – stopping from time to time to fight back tears – about the financial difficulties she had been going through and how her life had been complicated by the non-payment of her pension. The officer listened. He apologised to Alice for the inconvenience the non-payment of her pension had caused. Alice was directed to speak to one of the clerks in the office there who would address her issues immediately.

But when Alice sat down with one of the clerks, the situation was different. The clerk told her she had to offer the pension officer 'kolanut' if she wanted her case to be fast-tracked because *Oga* (the boss) would not sign any cheque 'just like that'. Alice clearly understood the message and she was determined to fight for her right. The clerk saw that Alice's jaw was set, and was ready for a fight. And when she said she was too poor to offer them any 'kolanut', the clerk went to the pension officer, apparently, to tell him what Alice had said. The officer invited Alice back to his office. He promised that within a week Alice would receive a cheque for all the money owed to her. Alice gave the pension officer the address of her daughter in Benin City where she expected to receive the cheque by post.

Alice went back to Benin City, clinging to hope of returning to some normal life.

But one week passed. Two weeks passed. Alice's cheque never came and now she had become an irritant to her son-in-law.

'Patricia! When will your mother go back to Lagos?' Julius said.

'What kind of question is that?'

'I just want her to go.'

'If she doesn't ...'

'Then I have to move out.'

'Come on, Julius! Are you out of your mind?'

'It's interesting how you've devoted yourself to conversation with your mum since she arrived here. And nobody else matters in the house.'

'Julius, are you a baby? My mum is going through a crisis period in her life. She needs our support.'

'I don't care, if you understand what I mean.'

'But you know she hasn't got a place to return to in Lagos.'

'You have to sort that out with her.'

Alice overheard part of the argument. She also heard Julius slam the front door as hard as he could when he stormed out of the house, leaving his breakfast on the table in the dining room.

'Pat! What's the matter?'

'Nothing's serious.'

'But Julius is very angry.'

'Mum, he just wants to know when you're going back to Lagos.'

'That won't be a problem, my dear.'

'Don't worry, mum, I'll calm him down.'

'Fine! But I'm not here to ruin your relationship with your husband. I notice that he hasn't been cheerful in the last couple of days. I think I've outstayed my welcome.'

Alice went back to her room. Her eyes were bright with unshed tears. She sat on the sofa and bent her head to her fate. Going back to Lagos without money seemed that the future was an abyss into which she would tumble and die.

'I'm going back to Lagos. If I can't get my pension, I'll die there.'

The following day, Alice went back to Lagos, and with no place of her own to return to, she went to a pub, drank herself to intoxication, and when it was dark, she shambled down to an abandoned house where she kept the night and there became her lodging for several weeks. Alice left the decrepit house after she had been beaten and sexually assaulted at night by some drunken men. With cardboard boxes, she made herself a home on the shoulder of a busy street near a heap of rubbish where she could browse for stale bread and avoid further sexual attack.

In the afternoon when the weather was hot and Alice was not wearing her top, her skin hung loosely on their bones; her dried breasts were pendulous; and the marks of the teeth of the cane of her attackers lined her body.

One afternoon, Alice had curled up inside her house of carton boxes. All her remaining possessions were in a pillow case she put under her head. The sky was overcast; the clouds pregnant with rain, swept over the rooftops and the whole city sank into darkness. When the rain started, it was unmerciful and somehow terrible. There was in it the primitive power of nature. It did not pour. It flowed. It was like a deluge from heaven, and rattled on the roofs of corrugated iron with a steady persistence that was maddening. The intensity of the rain sent animals and people on the streets scurrying for cover. Alice did not move, even after her home of cardboard boxes had been blown away like the chaff of wheat by the gusty wind which had accompanied the rain.

After the rain two local council officials visited Alice and urged her to leave the street. The rain had soaked through every layer of her clothing. She was shivering all over in a desperate effort to get warm. She grew colder and colder and now her teeth began to clatter. And quickly a large number of curious people had gathered to gawk. They thought Alice was mentally unhinged, or was a woman with evil spirits receiving her comeuppance in the end.

'We're here to help you,' one of the government officials said.

Alice stared at them with her brows drawn up. She spoke in a low voice with a spark of something that excited compassion, and her accents were educated.

'Who're you?'

‘We’re local council officials. We’re taking you away from here.’

‘I’m not going anywhere. I want to die here if I can’t get my pension.’

‘But we won’t let you die here.’

‘Listen to me! I’ve got nothing to live for. Our government is owing to me six months’ unpaid retirement pension. I have just heard that the pensions minister is involved in a massive pension fraud scheme amounting to more than N100 billion. I’m a nurse midwife. I served this country for thirty-five years. This is a poor substitute for my service to this nation. So let me die here if I can’t get my pension, I repeat.’

When Alice had finished, people around her opened their mouths with astonishment. They listened to how she had spoken English fluently, with a copious choice of words, and how she had put what she had to say plainly and with logical sequence. The tear of sympathy began to communicate from person to person with congenial speed. Immediately, some people were rushing here and there to provide Alice with food and a blanket to keep her warm.

‘This is unbelievable!’ One man in the crowd said with a sudden surge of emotion. ‘And we call this corrupt country “the giant of Africa?” Give me a break! This woman must have worked hard all her life to give life to so many babies. And the irony of all is that she may have been the midwife who helped bring some of these corrupt officials into this world.’

Now, the two local council officials, realizing that Alice’s case could become big news, hurriedly went back to the office to share Alice’s story with their superiors.

Later in the evening, Alice’s picture and her story appeared in several organs of the press. Most evening papers called for the immediate dismissal of the chairman of the pension board, and for a thorough investigation to be launched into what they said was 'a crying shame that a retired civil servant is ending her days in penury and starvation in the street because of unpaid pension'.

As the news swept through the nation like a forest fire, some prominent government officials visited Alice with apologies. They promised that Alice would be paid all her pension arrears within seven working days. Hope suddenly surged through Alice. And she finally agreed to leave the street. As she struggled to get up from her position on the ground, the officials helped her to her feet. She looked so thin that it seemed as if her clothes were holding her together.

Alice was taken away in an ambulance under police escort to hospital. But worries about the home she would return to immediately after her discharge from hospital kept boggling her mind. But the day she left hospital, she received her cheque, and she was moved to a well-furnished-one-bedroom flat, rent-free.

Goodbye To Russia

'*Обезьяна*'/abizia:na/ (monkey) was the first word of Russian I came across in Moscow a few years ago. The word was spoken by a young man outside Sheremetyevo Airport. I came to know the meaning of the word two months later when the police used it several times during a raid on a one-bedroom flat occupied by a group of African migrants in Mytishchi, a poor suburb of Moscow. This incident and many more violated my expectations of the country.

I travelled to Russia because I had been offered admission to study ship-building and navigation at Murmansk State Technical University, Murmansk. I saw this as a great opportunity to gain freedom, through education, in one of the most powerful countries on earth. On the day I got my Russian visa, I was rolling on the floor to celebrate. And I became the recipient of many congratulations from friends and family.

The day I arrived in Moscow, it was in the afternoon. When I came out of the airport, I felt I was setting foot in a different world. I took time to admire the surroundings which were spick and span. I saw high-rise glass buildings, sparkling in the sunlight. The grass in the area was cut nice and smooth. The hedges were trimmed and made flat on top like beds wrapped with green blankets. Tears of happiness welled up in my eyes. I stood still for a while to imagine what my life would look like away from my rustic village in Nigeria.

Now, it was time to begin the second phase of my journey from Moscow to Murmansk. I had no idea how to begin the transition. I opened my luggage and brought out the address of the university. As I was looking around to ask for directions, I saw two young Russian men standing in the shade of a tree opposite the airport. They looked like members of the military. They both had their hair cut short to their scalps. And they were clad in camouflage trousers, tucked into calf-length black combat boots. On top of the trousers, they were wearing black T-shirts with a red sign which looked like an 'S' intercrossing another 'S'. One of the men was smoking a cigarette with his eyes half closed and was tapping the cigarette ash into a metal litter bin, as a cloud of smoke from his nostrils and mouth was curling over his head. The other chap was taking tiny black seeds out of his trouser pocket, crushing them with his teeth, eating the wheat and spitting out the chaff.

'Good afternoon, guys,' I said, as I approached them.

'Sorry! No English,' one of them said, laughing derisively.

'*Abiziana*' the other one told me, pointing me back to the airport building.

Realizing that the two Russians were not helpful, I left and I was on my way back to the information desk when a couple in their thirties came up to me. I felt a surge of excitement when I saw that they were fellow Africans, particularly at that awkward moment in a foreign land.

'*Bonjour, mon frère*,' the man said.

My excitement began to wane at hearing another foreign language.

'I don't speak French,' I said.

'No problem, I speak small English,' he said, smiling.

'O, good! Where are you from?' I said.

'Cameroon.'

'And you?'

'Nigeria.'

'*A bon*! I know Nigeria. I'm Tanko. This is my girlfriend, Flabin. We're students in Patrick Lumumba University, Moscow.'

'I'm James. I'm happy to meet you,' I said, shaking hands with them.

Tanko was a sturdy broad-shouldered fellow, and of medium height. He was dark in complexion. He had a well-kept moustache which he constantly stroked. There was a roll of fat at the back of his neck. His face was caved in as if it had been smashed with a heavy blow. Tanko was clad in slip-on boat shoes; a pair of jean trousers, washed to a pale blue like the colour of the sky after a rain shower; a white polo shirt and a white baseball cap corked to one side of his head. Overall, there was in his appearance an air of good nature and in his vigour a glow of health that instantly gave you confidence.

Flabin was about five feet six. She had a short upper lip and an engaging smile which exposed her regular and very white teeth. She wore her hair in beautiful braids in straight lines like a column radiator. She was dressed in a white shirt above a blue ruffled skirt, a choker necklace and T-strap leather shoes.

After exchanging greetings with the couple, I told them I had come to Russia to study. I brought out the address of the university, and I asked Tanko if he knew how I could get there. He looked at the address and said he had not heard of the university or its location. But he would not find it difficult locating the university town when we got to central Moscow. He suggested that I should stay in his place for a few days before travelling to my final destination. I could not suppress the exclamation of delight with which I accepted the invitation. But I told him that the need for my course registration would prevent me from spending more than a couple of nights with him. He said it was fine with him. I gladly followed Tanko and Flabin home.

When we arrived, and as soon as Tanko opened the front door, I felt stifled by an acrid smell that rose from unwashed dishes in the kitchen sink. The smell reminded me of a hencoop.

'James! Come in. Come in.'

There were two rooms in the apartment. In one of them, I heard voices of more than two people chattering. Tanko took me into the other room he shared with Flabin. He put my luggage in a corner, and provided me with a place to hang my suit. As soon as Tanko and Flabin left me alone in the room, I craned my neck to look for any evidence of student-related activities. On one side of the room, I saw a small table with legs like a twisted wheel of a horse-drawn carriage. I was still looking when Tanko called me.

'*Mon frère*, come.'

Tanko took me to the bathroom. He showed me how to use the two faucets underneath a shower head, and after wasting a lot of water, I managed to adjust the water temperature for a warm shower. When I finished, Flabin had set the table for dinner. It was *fufu* with a soup, rich in legumes and assorted internal animal organs. After the meal, I praised Flabin's cooking, and I thanked Tanko for making the delicious dinner possible. Not long after that a sense of drowsiness invaded my veins. Words began to cut in my mouth, and the intervals between them became longer. In the mid-sentence I sank onto the mattress which Tanko had laid on the floor for me, and I quickly succumbed to the soporific effect of my full belly.

The following morning, when I opened my eyes, I saw that someone had tampered with my luggage. I leapt up to check and was relieved that my school fees – one thousand dollars in Thomas Cook traveller's cheques – still remained intact. I reached for my wallet in the breast pocket of my suit and I discovered that two hundred dollars was missing, leaving me with a hundred dollars. 'Shit! How can these guys do this to me?' I gave a gasp of anger, but I permitted myself to be regulated by coolness and temper. It would be folly to bandy hot words with my hosts, as I still needed Tanko's help to continue my journey. However, I called Tanko and told him what had happened.

'Tanko!'

'Yes, *mon frère*.'

'Two hundred dollars is missing from my wallet.'

'*C'est pas vrai*!'

Tanko swelled like a great bullfrog.

'You think we steal your money?'

Tanko called Flabin and told her in French what I had said. Flabin looked at me with a frown.

'Why?' she said, 'we do you good. You do us bad. Why?'

'Tanko, I must leave today,' I said. 'Thank you very much for your help.'

'*C'est bon pour nous*!'

I felt sorely disappointed in these fellow Africans. Later that day I took my luggage and followed Tanko to the city centre. We located the station where I caught a train to Murmansk.

***

I arrived in Murmansk the following afternoon. The beauty of the town took my breath away. Murmansk State Technical University is along Sportivnaya Street, and within walking distance from the train station. Its buildings, many of which are joined together like a chain, were buried in a jungle of Norway spruce. The presence of the spruce reminded me of Christmas time. The campus smelt of trees, sweet-smelling flowers, and the sea. On one side of the campus, I noticed that there were some rocky peaks jutting above the trees. The look of the woods and the rare smell of them renewed my blood and the intensity of interest to study there.

Here was a fresh experience. I saw birds in their gay plumage and brilliant butterflies fluttering around. It was amazing to see the incredible chemistry between man and animals, as collared pigeons and blackbirds were busy with their own affairs – mating, playing, and pecking stuff for lunch – without the fear that they might be harassed by passers-by. In Nigeria no birds as big as woodpigeons, even when they sit on top of the tallest tree, can feel safe from hunters' Dane guns or catapults. Murmansk seemed to offer me a smiling welcome.

Now, I made my way to the registrar's office. The name of the registrar was Boris. I introduced myself to him as a potential new student. He got up from his seat and stretched his hand towards me for a handshake. His hands were hairy and his arms were like tree trunks. He was big and stout with a mass of grey hair around a high dome of bald head, bushy eyebrows and an enormous ginger moustache. He had a deep bass voice and he spoke English unerringly. He made me welcome to Murmansk.

Boris took me to the hostel where he introduced to me two African students – in their second year. Their rooms were opposite the room I would be living in. He told them to help me as much as they could. He made them understand that it would be helpful to have them around me while I was still getting to know the university environment.

Later that afternoon Boris took me to the canteen. It was as if he knew that my empty stomach had been waiting for more than twelve hours for a small portion of food. He spoke with one member of the canteen staff who quickly heaped a soup-plate with brown rice and two large crayfish and placed it in front of me. I ran my tongue out to wet my lips as the plate was being set before me. The plate was piled high in the shape of a pyramid. In no time, I ate up the rice. And as I began to suck fat out of the heads of the crayfish, Boris left and returned to his office. But as he was leaving, he told me to come to his office the following morning for registration.

The following morning after breakfast, I went to see Boris in his office.

'Good morning, Boris.'

'Morning, James. Do you have your passport with you?'

I dipped my hand into the breast pocket of my suit jacket and gave him my documents.

'Ok. We are going to the immigration office for your stay permit.'

Boris drove me to the immigration office. Before long, I was issued a three-month temporary stay permit.

While I was still there, a man called me into his office. His name was Mikhail. He was tall. He had a straggly beard on his thin face. When he laughed, he displayed long brown teeth. I did not know what had happened to him, but that morning he carried a crutch under his left arm, and he appeared to be still weak from his apparent injury. He greeted me warmly. He asked me if I was ready to work for the authorities. I answered in the affirmative, even though I had no idea yet what the nature of the job would be. He thanked me for agreeing to work for them, and he promised to come to my hostel the next day to see me. I went back that moment feeling happy that I had landed a job to support my studies. I was dead wrong.

When Mikhail came to me the following day, he asked me if I had met the two African students whose rooms were opposite mine. I told him I had met them. He said my task was to spy on them. He told me to make it my business to know what they did on a daily basis, including the time they went out and came in. He gave me a pseudonym –Jack –, and a secret code number. He took me to an old phone booth at the back of my hostel, with the instruction to dial the code at 4pm every day to keep him informed about my spy targets. When he turned his back, a broad grin broke on my lips and I put my thumb to my nose and cocked a snook at him. I asked myself: 'Why would this man or the so-called 'authorities' feel that those African students would be a security risk to the university?' And something within me told me loud and clear that the same students must have also been told to monitor my own activities, too. But, as it happened, I had no way of knowing how the 'authorities' would have reacted if I refused to spy on the students because my own registration to start my studies in the university had been unsuccessful.

Trouble started when my traveller's cheques could not be cashed in Murmansk to pay for my studies. There were two big banks in Murmansk. But none of them accepted the cheques. The university sent them to its bank in Helsinki, Finland. They were returned two weeks later with a letter, stating that I should have been present to sign the cheques in the presence of the bank cashiers. That effectively dashed my hopes. And all of a sudden my heart began to behave strangely. Like a rocket set off, it began to leap and expand into uneven patterns of beats which showered into my brain. I felt like the earth should open and swallow me whole. My eyes smarted with dry tears. And with nothing else to do, the university decided that I should go back to Nigeria.

'Dream shattered!'

Two days later after breakfast, I sat at a front window in my room. I found myself thinking of all the things I could do to cheer me up. I took my camera and I went to the city centre at about three o'clock in the afternoon to take some photos in remembrance of my short stay in Murmansk. That afternoon the air was warm and still. I went to the seaside to feel cool wind; watch a great number of seagulls moaning overhead, flying close to the shore; and the surf tumbling and tossing its foam on the sandy beach.

At nine, after taking some night pictures of the city, I decided to take a taxi to the hostel because it was too dark for me to walk alone. I sat in the back of the cab. The driver and one other man sat in the front. I was driven to the foot of a mountain, dragged out, and beaten. The force of the blows to my face made me giddy. I felt an acute pain under my left eye as if I had been stabbed. Blood was welling up from my gaping wound. I was robbed of my camera, shoes, and a wallet containing thirty dollars. When my attackers left, I shambled down to a nearby log house, where I met an elderly woman. She saw my chest heaving as I struggled unsuccessfully to explain to her in her native language what had happened to me. She knew instantly that I had been attacked and that I must be a student in the only university there. She talked to me in Russian, but I did not understand anything. She went inside and when she came out she beckoned to me to follow her. She led me to the university campus.

That night Boris was called in. He took me to the police station where photos of some local congenital hooligans were shown to me to see if I could identify my attackers. My eyelids had closed over my eyes, and my whole face swelled as if I had been stung by a bee. I was unable to identify anybody and I told the police so. After they made a few fruitless enquiries, the police took me to hospital. But within ten minutes I was sent back to the hostel to bleed some more, as I was not given any treatment. The deep cut under my eye was not even patched up.

I woke up the next morning with my nose caked in dry blood and with a pounding headache. When Boris came to see me that morning, he brought me an exit visa to go back home. He gave me a hundred dollars and a train ticket to Moscow.

***

When I arrived back in Moscow, I had no idea where I could lay my head for the night. But as I came out of Komsomolskaya train station, I saw four black men in a bus shelter. A pain was still chewing through my swollen face. I explained to them how I had been beaten and robbed in Murmansk. I told them I wanted a place to stay for a couple of days to treat myself before going back to Nigeria.

Two of the men (Meyers and Francis) took me to their one bedroom apartment in Mytishchi. The flat stank of stale air. The rust on window frames showed that the windows had not been opened for a long time, which denied the flat the exposure to fresh air. I was introduced to five men I met there. None of them was pleased to see me join them. Meyers told me afterwards that the men were not happy because the flat was already overcrowded. He was right, you see. By bedtime, the number of the occupants had increased to seventeen. It was so crowded that the kitchen, bathroom and toilet were used at night as sleeping spaces. And it was so noisy that I could not tear myself away from the noise until it departed of its own accord after most of the boys had fallen asleep. And while they were asleep, I could not sleep because I was heavily oppressed by the unpleasant smells that rose from their bodies.

Seriously speaking, those African migrants were living in squalor. No one had a job. I was not sure if any of them could afford more than one meal a day. Some were living on stale bread, dipped in *молоко* /moloko/ (milk) with a little sugar in it. Most of these African migrants had come to Russia for the same reason as I had.

One evening in the flat, everybody had arrived back from the city. Those who could afford it were cooking their dinner in the kitchen. Some people were munching on tart apples and wormy plums for the night. Those who were ready to sleep on empty stomachs, but whose sleeping space was the busy kitchen, were watching a movie on a black-and-white TV placed on a small well-polished table made from hard native wood somewhat like mahogany in one corner of the room.

Suddenly, there was a determined knock at the door followed by a shout of the word: 'abizia:na, abizia:na. Silence descended on the flat. But the knock continued, this time with another word: 'politsiya'. A man who spoke Russian fairly well among us went to answer the door. He opened it, but left it on the latch in order to identify who was there.

'They're policemen,' he announced.

When the door was finally unbolted, two men in police uniform and three men in mufti rushed in. The policemen pulled their pistols from their waists and ordered everyone to take his bag with him. They shuffled us to one side. Everyone had his bag ransacked. Those who had raw cash and other valuable items lost them. One of the policemen found my traveller's cheques stapled together. He looked at them. He then passed the cheques to his colleagues. My heart began to hammer in my chest. I think they must have been disappointed that the cheques were not raw cash, as the last man who examined them squeezed them and bunged them on the floor. I was lucky. They did not take them or tear them up. Immediately they left, I picked the cheques up and ironed a few that were crumpled.

'This is not the first time they've come here, robbing us and calling us 'abizia:na,' Meyers said.

'What does 'abizia:na' mean?' I asked.

'Oh! You mean you don't know? It's "monkey",' Meyers said.

I slapped my head. This was the moment I realized that my quality as a human being had been terribly degraded by one of the two Russian men who said the same word to me at the airport on the day I arrived in Russia. Now, I wanted nothing more than to leave the country. Every other consideration suddenly left me.

'It isn't safe to live here.' I said.

The only concern I had was whether or not I could find a bank in Moscow to cash my cheques because that was the only means of getting out before my exit visa expired.

Let me put that concern aside for a second. There was another incident whose nature and paraphernalia seemed much larger than those of the incidents which happened to me in Murmansk. I have never ceased to be surprised that it happened in Moscow. I shall venture to request a few minutes to talk about it.

A week after the police raid on our flat, I accompanied Meyers to a business centre in Taganskaya where stranded

African migrants usually made calls to their friends and relatives for financial help. The centre also served as a place where those in desperate need of human kindness could find some American Christian charity organizations to provide them with food and clothing. We left the centre with five other men before it was dark. When we got off the bus somewhere, I cannot remember the name of the place now, we saw six Russian youths raining blows on the head of a black man. At one point the man broke into a run, but not for long. His attackers caught him and kicked him about the head, even when he was now down. I noticed right away that the men were dressed like those I met at the airport.

Near the scene, there were two officers of the law standing by their vehicle. One would expect them to do the needful – stand for law and order and protect the man under attack against that horde of ruthless criminals. Instead, they were watching and enjoying the fun. My mouth fell open. To tell you the truth, it would be an unusually callous person who would not feel his blood boil at such malignant treatment of a defenseless migrant. Fury blazed in the eyes of Meyers and four other men with me. They saw the overwhelming necessity to save the life of the man, and they were ready to do battle until the end of their strength. I was still too weak to join any fight.

Quickly, two of the Russians were wrestled to the ground as the Africans got the upper hand. Now the Russians were bleeding and the police saw fit to intervene. And this was the time the black man under attack, having lost two front teeth, managed to scuttle away on all fours.

One elderly man, who had been watching with some embarrassment, was horrified at this spectacle of lawlessness. He scratched his chin which was just beginning to sprout a beard, and then came up to me and said with emotion:

'I don't like this in my country, but one man can't win a war.'

I felt my eyes prick with tears.

The next day, Meyers and I went to a big bank in Arbatskaya. I took one of my traveller's cheques with me. At the bank, I met a neatly dressed young lady cashier whose charming face was wreathed in smiles. I smiled at her, and she at me. She had large blue eyes that looked as though they were made of glass. Her firm, round breasts rose proudly as she leaned over the counter before me. I gave the cheque which she took inside with her. After about ten minutes, she called me and asked me to sign the cheque. I got the first one hundred dollars. Before leaving the bank, I told the cashier that I had more cheques to clear, explaining that they were meant to be cashed to pay for my studies, but I had now decided to go back to Africa. I went back the following day to clear the rest of the cheques.

Instead of going back to the university in Murmansk with the money, I bought a one-way ticket for the next available flight to Nigeria. I gave one hundred and fifty dollars to Meyers to pay his rent. A week later, I bade goodbye to Russia.

The State Of The Nation

I am not sure whether I should describe Robinson Ire as a disturbed young man who unconsciously annulled his pain by inflicting it on other creatures. Or I should say he is a product of a disturbed nation.

Robinson's eyes were red as he came out of a job interview room in Lagos. Outside, he spotted a kitten, curled up with its eyes half-closed. Robinson kicked the animal in the head against a brick wall and, as the poor creature was on its way to dying, he strolled blithely out of view.

Robinson was twenty-three years old. He was of medium height, heavily built and light in complexion. Instantly noticeable about him was the closeness with which his eyes were set. He was born of humble parents, with a teacher for a father and a nurse for a mother. His father died of inoperable cancer when he was fifteen. He had lived with his parents in a well-furnished two-bedroom flat in Ikeja, but after the death of his father, the family fell on hard times. His mother, Joyce, could not afford the rent by herself and she moved to an abandoned house on the outskirts of Lagos where she paid low rent for two rooms in return for taking care of the house.

The house was incredibly dingy. At night, the mad dash of rats from door to door was of an Olympic standard. It appeared as if the house had acted as a meeting place for mice and a breeding ground for the insect population. There were cockroaches the size of small mice everywhere. And poisonous hairy spiders weaved their webs in every corner of the rooms. Later the presence of Robinson and his mother reduced the population of the rodents, but it did little to scare the spiders away. It was here Robinson lived with his mother who scrimped and saved to fund his university education. Joyce believed that her son would be able to improve the quality of their lives when he found a good job after university.

Robinson's latest interview was the twenty-fifth attempt at getting a job since he graduated four years ago. When he arrived back home, he called his mother.

'Mum, it's bad news again. I didn't get the job.'

Joyce slapped her head.

'God, have mercy! Something is wrong with this country.'

One morning Robinson woke up and, with nothing to eat for breakfast, went to the industrial area of Lagos to see if he could be hired by a company for a low-paid manual job. That same morning, Joyce took her cutlass to clear the weeds around the house. Hardly had she started when she was stung in the face by a brown 'recluse' spider. She did not immediately realize the dangerous effect of the bite until she began to throw up with chronic abdominal pain hours later. By the time Robinson arrived home later in the afternoon, Joyce was in a critical condition, her face had swollen badly. Her tongue had swollen to twice its size, and when she tried to move it, it stuck horribly to the roof of her mouth. And her head was pounding.

Robinson rushed his mother to hospital. He was shocked to realize that there was not even anti-venom drug with which to treat his mother. He would need to buy the drug from the private drugstore of the hospital's chief medical doctor. He rushed back home to his mother's room for money. He found nothing. He dashed back to the hospital and pleaded with the doctor on duty.

‘Please doctor! Save my mother’s life.’

‘We don’t have anti-venom. And there’s nothing I can do,’ the doctor said, walking away from Robinson.

Robinson went back home. His face was puffy having spent the whole afternoon crying his eyes out in the hospital. He sat on the floor in his room and bent his head to his lap.

‘God, where is your kindness? My mother must not die!’

Darkness was gathering. Robinson sprang to his feet. An idea came to his head. He went to a coach station where he spent the night helping travellers to unload goods from, or to load goods onto trucks for a pittance. He did find enough money to buy his mother anti-venom for her treatment, but it was too late. When he rushed back to the hospital with the medicine the following morning, Joyce had died. Robinson went wild. He jingled like a cymbal. He whistled like a flute. He beat his chest and upended tables. He stormed the ward and disturbed patients lying in their beds.

A few months after the burial of his mother, Robinson began to fall behind with the rent, and his tenancy was now in danger. One afternoon, he opened a carton box, brought out all the rejection letters to his job applications and spread them open on the table as if inviting God Himself to read them. He took his backpack and went into the kitchen. He put into his bag a seven-inch-long knife which shone as though it had just come out of the smith’s workshop. He zipped up the bag, slung it over his shoulder and set out for coach stations and began to mug women traders.

Robinson soon joined a highway robbery gang, attacking passengers travelling on long-distance buses along the East/West Road at night. The first raids he took part in were financially successful without hurting anyone and when the money was shared out at the house of the ringleader, Robinson netted $5,000. When he got home he threw wads of money into the air to celebrate. 'Where was money like this when my mother was dying?'

Robinson paid his arrears of rent. He travelled to South Africa to enjoy the rest of his money.

On his return, he took part in more robbery operations before undergoing musketry training in the East with a group of militants agitating for the creation of their own Republic. After his training, Robinson would brag among his gang members about his ability to shoot off the end of a cigarette from the hip, or shoot a pipe from a man's mouth without causing him an injury. He formed his own five-man robbery gang with its headquarters in Lagos. He recruited a number of informants to work at coach stations. Their job was to inform Robinson and his gang about traders who could be carrying large amounts of money and the coaches they were travelling on.

Robinson's first personally-supervised robbery operation was ugly, as two men were killed on a coach travelling from Anambra to Lagos. The victims had resisted parting with their money. Robinson would not let that happen. He pulled the trigger of his AK47 rifle, and when the barrel of the gun cracked the air, the two passengers lay dead on the aisle of the bus. Their coach had run into a roadblock set up at night by Robinson and his gang. By the time the police arrived, all they could see were the cooling bodies of the victims lying heavy and lifeless. The raids netted the gang $45,000, and the bandits made a clean getaway.

After the incident, Robinson and his gang thought it best to lie low. But the lull did not last longer than two weeks. As Robinson could find his victims so easily, he passed from one hunting ground to another, leaving behind scars of atrocities across town after town. The Lagos State Intelligence and Investigations Bureau chief, Superintendent William said:

'Robinson is the most notorious criminal I've ever had to deal with in my 27 years in the police force.'

Superintendent William and his team could not lay their hands on Robinson. They could only learn that he had been in some area when, having done his work, he had left it. The trouble was that the police did not have Robinson's true identity. Robinson himself knew it.

The next bloody robbery attack took place in broad daylight in Lagos where Robinson and his men heavily armed and wearing balaclavas had successfully raided a bank. From the time the gang entered the bank to the time they came out with a huge amount of money only fifteen minutes elapsed.

The operation put the gang in close contact with the police on vehicle patrol, and a large-scale gunfight followed. Robinson and his men gained the upper hand, as an inspector and three of his men were shot dead. As the bandits were making their escape from the scene, they threw bundles of local currency to the cheering crowds, including school children who were returning home that afternoon.

Following the killing of the police officers by Robinson and his men, the police launched the greatest manhunt for Robinson in the city. But he had slipped through the border to The Republic of Benin to allow things to cool down at home. Superintendent William could only clench his fists in frustration.

'If only I can capture Robinson, dead or alive, I can afford to ignore members of his gang.'

When Robinson returned, and while still waiting for things to cool down, he attended The Eyo Festival. The usual open air musical concert of the Festival makes it of compelling interest for young people, including foreign tourists. Robinson was there to shadow wealthy people he could one day attack. As his gaze was wandering around, it settled on a tall, good-looking lady in her thirties. In the midst of her friends, she was dancing and rotating her hips like a Congolese dancing girl. Robinson winked at her and she smiled. It was not immediately clear whether Robinson was in the sway of the devil within him and was thinking of the lady as his next victim. Or he suddenly fell head over heels in love, which conquers all. Anyway, Robinson went up to the lady and struck up an acquaintance with her.

'Hi, I'm George Okereke,' Robinson said, assuming a false name.

'I'm Christina,' the lady said, turning her brown eyes that danced with merriment, and with an infectious smile that touched Robinson.

After a small chit-chat, Robinson and Christina agreed to meet again when the Festival was over.

A couple of weeks later, Robinson set out on a date with Christina. It was one Saturday afternoon. The sun was shining brightly under the cloudless sky. When Robinson arrived to take her out, Christina was still making up her face; her mouth rolling the lipstick onto her lips, while her eyes were rolling around in the mirror.

'Are you ready?' Robinson said.

'Where are you taking me?'

Robinson was wearing a linen suit with a striped shirt, opened at the collar that exposed to view his hairy and virile chest. No tie. Robinson took Christina to Eko Holiday Inn the back of which faces the Atlantic Ocean. When Robinson and Christina entered the hotel, their nostrils were filled with a hint of *isi ewu* stew. The couple sat in the garden at the back of the hotel. It was surrounded by a low wooden fence on top of which there were creeping plants resting their flowering hands, and here and there, were beds of roses. They sat down at a table under a beach umbrella. Although the weather was hot, it was tempered with the cool breeze blowing across from the Atlantic Ocean, fluttering the leaves of the surrounding trees. As Robinson and Christina took their seats, a waiter appeared with the menu and took their orders.

When the bill arrived, Christina looked on in astonishment as Robinson peeled fifty dollar notes from the substantial wad he kept in his wallet. After the meal, Robinson briefly re-introduced himself to Christina. He rested his hand on Christina's and gave it an affectionate squeeze.

'Thank you for coming here with me.

'Thanks for the meal,' Christina said, as a slow smile moved her lips.

'I think we can start a good relationship. I'm single. I buy and sell second-hand vehicle parts, and I base in Accra, Ghana.'

Having listened with rapt attention, Christina said:

'Hmm. George, you can't make a fool of me, right. How can you keep a relationship steady in Nigeria while you live and do your business in Ghana?'

'No! I've always wanted to relocate to Lagos.'

There was an agreeable twinkle in Christiana's black shinning eyes.

'Well, I'm a single mum. I work in the Federal Ministry of Mines and Power, here in Lagos. My husband died in a car accident on his way to the office three years ago. I have a five-year-old son, Jackson,' she said with a voice tinged with emotion.

Robinson pulled Christina into his arms and parted her in the back.

'Now I can see the image of my mum in your eyes. She raised me alone after the death of my father.'

Christina simply felt womanly. She would like a man (not too handsome to attract other women) to take her on his lap and pet her and cuddle her and call her little baby names. And she seemed to think that on a Sunday afternoon she should be taken for a walk. Robinson seemed to fit in.

Three months into their relationship, Robinson and Christiana were affianced. Robinson moved Christina and her son, who had been living in a single room, into a three-bedroom two-storey house in a secluded area of Lagos. He furnished the house. He gave Jackson a separate room. He shared a room with Christina downstairs while he kept the only room upstairs for his personal use.

One evening after dinner, Robinson stretched his arms, yawed and bade Christina and Jackson good night. He went into his private room upstairs. Instead of going to bed, he stayed awake on the sofa throughout the night, thinking about his next move. He rang all his criminal gang members, and the following day, they assembled at their hideout.

Robinson's boys respected him a lot because his criminal brain worked at lightning speed. He was regarded as a competent leader who knew his job from A to Z. They had implicit faith in him, for he planned their every move. Before setting off for his operation, Robinson had timed everything to the minute and every move had been well-rehearsed. Every man knew his place and every man took it, and when the job was done, it was done with the art of a master. Robinson's uncanny ability to do a job without leaving a trace earned him the nickname '*The Invisible*' among his boys.

Now, Robinson and his gang started kidnapping politicians and wealthy businessmen and women, who attracted attention to themselves by extravagance. Robinson rented a house on the outskirts of the city to hide away his victims. He bought himself three mobile phones: one, for calling his members; another, for calling his girlfriend, Christina; and the other, for calling his victims' families for the payment of ransoms.

Another of Robinson's brutal attacks took place on a Christmas Eve. The Christian world was alive with Christmas spirit. Mothers preparing holiday feasts and wrapping gifts, and children waiting in expectation of the visit of Santa Claus. That day Robinson kidnapped the head of a family who had just bought a wild goat for the Christmas celebration. He was on his way home with the animal when Robinson and his gang attacked his car, seized him violently, blindfolded him and bundled him and the animal into their van and sped off. A few days after the gang had received $80,000 ransom paid by the victim's family and friends, his battered remains were found hidden in dense undergrowth in Ikeja, a necklace of ugly bruises staining his neck, and rough gags stuffed into his mouth.

Kidnapping was bad enough, but killing a victim after a huge ransom had been paid was a new kind of atrocity the public found hard to deal with. The press was in full cry. Reporters were running out of adjectives to describe the on-going saga of killing, kidnapping and robbery. One of them remarked:

'We need a new language.'

The blazing flames of criticism from the press against the police consumed the Lagos State Police Commissioner who was instantly removed for dereliction of duty by the Inspector General of Police. A new police chief offered a large reward for any information that could lead to Robinson's arrest. Superintendent William and his team, highway patrol officers, members of the Directorate of State Service (DSS), and urban police departments all combined into a veritable army to defeat this elusive enemy. But the net result of all this effort proved futile. William and his team began to round up vagrants, and scores of innocent people were kept in police stations for hours and days, answering questions levelled at them by these tired detectives working under pressure from their new commissioner.

Two weeks of enquiry passed in this way, producing mountains of paperwork and a vast ocean of frustration. No genuine advance was made, and some cynics wondered whether so much adverse criticism and disappointment had made the investigators give up on Robinson and his gang.

Now, Robinson's notoriety had soared, and yet his facial features had not been known to the authorities – a source of terrible nightmares for the police and the public at large. Wealthy men began to form their own vigilante groups to provide themselves with security. And women of substance had no realistic option but to hire bodyguards or huddle for safety behind locked doors.

So far Robinson had received millions of dollars as ransom from his victims. He bought himself a Lexus SUV, and a beautiful turnkey house in the middle of a handsome area in Lagos. He bought his girlfriend, Christina, a Toyota Camry. As he became more infatuated with Christina, he began to spend quality time with her at home and allow the seething anger of the public and police against him to subside.

Captured at last? The police got the vital clue that had eluded them for months when a teacher, Julius Agogo, escaped from Robinson's custody in the middle of the night. Julius had been held for two months because his ransom of a million dollars had not been paid by his family. Police had tried in vain to find him when the news of his kidnap was first published in the newspaper. Wearing a grimy pair of jeans, a sleeveless vest, and looking as if he had not had a bath for weeks, Julius had run barefoot to the city and straight to the police station. Julius was physically shaking with beads of sweat on his forehead.

'I've some important information for the commissioner of police, please,' he said.

The inspector on duty was eager to have the information, but Julius refused, as he was not sure if any secret cooperation existed between the police in the area and Robinson and his gang. The duty officer immediately contacted the Divisional Police Officer. Early in the morning, Julius was driven to the Lagos State Police headquarters, Ikeja, and straight to the commissioner's office.

'Young man, how may I help you?' the police boss said.

'I'm Julius Agogo, kidnapped by Robinson and his men two months ago.'

'Do you know him physically?'

'I'd been in his custody for two months, and he'd talked to me twice without wearing a mask.'

The Commissioner leaned back in his chair, took off his glasses and wiped them. He put them back on. He took his mobile phone and called the Inspector General of Police in Abuja, the nation's capital. The police chief instructed the Commissioner to keep the teacher in a safe location and warned him not to breathe a word about the development to the press. The Commissioner took Julius to the police officers' mess. A large contingent of antiriot policemen was stationed there to provide security. The Commissioner immediately sent for Superintendent William who arrived with his team and with a small group of fingerprint experts and artists to talk to Julius who recalled the visual observations he had made about Robinson.

After Julius had given the law officers an approximate age of Robinson and his detailed facial description, the police constructed the identikit picture of their man. It was shown to Julius who agreed that it was an excellent sketch of the man who had kept him away from his family for months.

Armed with the identikit of their man, the police, taking Julius with them, stormed the house used as the hideout of the criminals who had disappeared following the escape of Julius from their custody. Julius took the officers round the house surrounded by a high stone fence and showed them how he had managed to scale the fence and escaped. A thorough search of the house yielded the police a large cache of sophisticated arms and ammunition. The authorities did not immediately release the identikit of Robinson to the press because internal investigation was still on-going. Instead, the sketch, at the top of which was written 'THE MOST WANTED PERSON!' was sent to all police headquarters across the country to see if any suspects in police custody would know and recognize Robinson. And about five hundred policemen were mobilized to carry out a full-scale hotel-to-hotel search in Lagos. And checkpoints were set up across Lagos to screen drivers and passengers going out of the city.

The escape of Julius genuinely worried Robinson and his boys. But Robinson did not see why he had to leave town. He was confident that his facial features were not known to the police. He kept himself in the house he rented for his girlfriend, Christina. Throughout that day he spread himself out on a couch and watched TV to monitor the development. Nothing was reported about him.

But two days later, he woke up to 'breaking news' on NTA Channel, airing his face repeatedly. And all the daily newspapers had his identikit picture on the front page. Robinson gazed at TV. The veins on his forehead stood out like knotted cords. Christina was in the office that morning, and saw one of the newspapers. The pupils of her eyes dilated.

'Oh, my good God, this looks like the face of George!' she said to herself.

Christina's nerves were shattered. Her head twitched madly. Her hands shook with fury. She came out of the office to call '*George*'. His phone, for the first time, was switched off. Christina took her handbag and headed straight home.

'George! George!'

George had disappeared, leaving his room wide open and unkempt. Waves of voices beat and rumbled in Christina's ears as in an empty shell. She again looked at the facial sketch on the front page of her newspaper and resolved that it indeed belonged to her *George*. Her horrified senses suspected that her romance with the most wanted criminal in the country had drawn her to a bizarre situation to which she was now tied hand and foot. Christina dropped on the sofa. Tears welled up in her eyes and flowed down her cheeks, making tracks through her make-up.

Christina moved quickly with a copy of the day's newspapers, picked up her son from school, and then drove to the police headquarters.

'I'm here in respect of this man,' Christina said, pointing to the sketch on the paper.

Superintendent William was summoned. Sitting in front of the officer, Christina said:

'This sketch fits the face of my boyfriend's.'

'Is Robinson your boyfriend?'

'I know him as George Okereke.'

'Where's he now?'

'I don't know. But I left him at home this morning.'

After four hours of interrogation, William had no fault to find with Christina.

Now, police had spread their dragnets across the city and around Christina's house for any possible return of Robinson. When Robinson left his room that morning, he had moved to a local hotel to take refuge. Two days later in the middle of the night, Robinson called Christina, as no hotel was now safe.

'George! Where are you?' Christina said.

'Are you with police?'

'Why are you talking about police?'

'Is Jackson there with you?'

'He's sleeping.'

'Wake him up!'

'Ok, hold on,' Christina said, as she went to Jackson and nudged him gently. 'Jackson, wake up! George wants to talk to you.'

Wiping his face with the back of his hand, Jackson took the phone.

'*Uncle* George, where are you?'

'Who's with you in the house?'

'My mum'

'Ok. Give the phone back to your mum.'

'Christina! Open the gate. I'll be with you in ten minutes.'

'All right, then.'

Christina put on a T-shirt, a pair of jeans and flip-flops and rushed straight to the gate and waited for

‘*George*’. After fifteen minutes, Robinson sneaked into the house.

‘George! Where have you been?’ Christina said.

‘Please close the gate and go to bed. I’ll tell you in the morning.’

‘Where’s your car?’

‘With my mechanic,’ Robinson said, as he was rushing upstairs.

The detectives who had kept the area under round-the-clock surveillance spotted their man and quickly called for reinforcements, which included their heavy no-nonsense riot squad. Christina and Jackson, now fully awake, quickly moved out of the house to a safe custody of the police. Within ten minutes the shuffle of heavy police boots – *wom, wom, wom* – was heard on cobblestones around the house and a noisy bark of a dog crashed into the building. The whole house had been cordoned off by heavily armed policemen, led by Superintendent William. The people in the street, who had been kept awake by the blaring sirens of ambulances and police cars, were all at their front doors. Quick as a flash, Robinson sprang to his feet. He walked slowly to the windows and peeped through the curtains. He was not surprised to see a line of police cars with blue lights flashing, as he was now aware that his facial features were in public domain. He dashed downstairs.

‘Christina! Jackson!’ he shouted.

With Christina and her son nowhere to be found, Robinson went berserk. He felt he had been betrayed by Christina who had told him there was no police presence in the area. He kicked down Christina’s bedroom door and then began cutting a swathe of rampant destruction inside each room, ripping out the drawers, spewing their contents over the floors, smashing the light bulbs, even punching and kicking the walls. He raced back upstairs.

He took his pistol, stuck it into his jean waistband and dashed back downstairs again.

Robinson now fully surrounded, the police felt that it was in their own interest to capture him alive so that they could extract the information which might lead them to the arrest of his accomplices. William let out a call from his megaphone.

'Robinson, put up your hands and come out!'

But Robinson, who stayed at a vantage point behind the curtain of the window he had partly opened, responded by firing shots at the police. A bullet penetrated a police sergeant and it lodged near his spine. Superintendent William, Robinson's tormentor-in-chief, was hit in the knee. Robinson brought his full experience in weapon training to bear on this latest and the last battle of his life with the police. Swiftly, William's men began their full operation by firing nine tear gas canisters into the house.

As smokes engulfed the house, the officers invaded it, smashing through the front door with a battering ram. And a fusillade of shots followed as they advanced. Robinson jumped out through the back window, and as he was running away, a hail of bullets drove him to the ground with a groan, a terrible groan of pain. The early dew from the grass seeped into his denim trousers as he sank down into his knees before toppling sideways to stare up into the sky.

As every well has a bottom, Robinson came to the end of his criminal life, and to the end of his own life, too.

An Ache in My Chest

I was seventeen when I was lured into prostitution. My father died of a sudden illness when I was ten. My mother refused to remarry to preserve her undying love for him. The death of my father made everyday life a struggle for me and my mother. She owed a lot of money to a lot of people in order to send me to secondary school.

One afternoon I had just come back home from school. I saw my mother splitting firewood with an axe at the back of the house. Her energy was running low, as she was panting for breath.

'Mum! Stop it. Let me help you.'

My mother stopped to mop the sweat that was streaming down her face with the edge of her loose skirt.

'Endurance, you can't even lift the axe. Eat the two bananas in the kitchen. And go and see Pastor Anozie.'

Pastor Anozie was the head of the church my mother and I attended every Sunday. When I got to Pastor Anozie's house, he was praying for divine intervention on behalf of a couple who had been looking for the 'fruit of the womb' for years. He was literally trembling, stamping his feet on the floor like a child throwing a tantrum. I sat on the sofa in the living room until he finished.

'Endurance, it's good to see you. I sent for you,' the Pastor said, as a broad grin appeared on his face.

'That's why I'm here sir,' I said.

'In my private prayers, I always remember you and your mother. And God has asked me to help you. Many nice houses in this town belong to girls your age. They don't make their money in Nigeria. They live and work hard in places like Italy and Russia. You're a good singer and hair stylist. Don't you like to travel abroad?'

'Yes sir, but I don't have the opportunity.'

'Leave that to me. I just want you to agree. And I'll talk to your mother about it when we meet on Sunday after church service.'

I went back home that afternoon feeling that God had come down to me in the likeness of man. I explained to my mother what Pastor Anozie had told me. My mother dropped on her knees and thanked Jesus. And from that night I began to have a recurring dream about a beautiful house with a steep roof and mullion windows I could build for my mother in the future.

Three days later, my mother and I met Pastor Anozie after church service.

'Madam Janet, congratulations!' Pastor Anozie said. 'I'm sending Endurance to Russia. I've spoken to my sister in Moscow. She'll help her find a job that pays well.'

'Pastor, may God bless you,' my mother said, as a smile broke on her lips.

We had not left the church premises when Pastor Anozie's phone rang.

'That's my sister from Moscow,' he said. 'Come and talk to her.'

On the merit of my conversation with Pastor Anozie's sister who introduced herself to me as Elizabeth, I got my passport. And a week before I travelled to Lagos to meet somebody who would arrange for my visa and ticket to Moscow, I went to see Elizabeth's mother who lived on the outskirts of Benin City. When she saw me, a broad smile spread over her wrinkled face and stayed there for the most part of the time. She was in the garden feeding one of her pigs who had given birth to a horde of small squeaking piglets. The other pigs were busy tilling the soil with their snouts, even if they did not have the objectives of sowing seeds.

'You're Endurance!'

'Yes ma. Good afternoon.'

'I'm Alice, Anozie's mother.'

Madam Alice, having brushed off some bits from her green garden apron, closed and padlocked the door of the garden.

'Wait here for me,' she said.

Madam Alice went into the house. And when she came out, she beckoned to me to follow her. She took me deep into the forest. It was windy. We went past a river which was still high after the recent rain. The only noises in the area were those from the rushing river and little birds twittering and flitting from side to side. I jerked to a halt. I looked back, left and right.

'Where are we going?'

'Just follow me.'

We stopped at the bottom of a giant tree. Madam Alice knelt down and praised the tree, chanting incantations. When she finished, she turned to me and said:

'Take off your knickers for me.'

'My what!'

'You heard me well.'

Sweat broke out on my forehead. My heart began to pound inside my rib-cage like a drum beating the retreat. No. Not only that. As the wind roared in the trees, the surrounding leaves swayed rapidly. And I felt like there were snatching hands of evil spirits ready to grab me. My throat tightened as I said:

'Why?'

'You must take a loyalty oath before you go to Moscow.'

As I heard the name 'Moscow' again, my heartbeat slowly returned to normal.

'All right,' I said, as I took off my knickers and gave them to her.

And in return, Madam Alice gave me scissors.

'What're they for?'

'Cut me a small quantity of your pubic hair.'

Now, believe me. I felt my blood freeze in my veins. But knowing that I would be going abroad to make a fortune and come back home to start a new life, weighed heavily against any attempt to deny the request.

Madam Alice put the hair into a small container like a salt cellar. Then she nailed my knickers to the giant tree.

'Now you can go. Don't betray my daughter in Moscow.'

'Madam, how do I go home without knickers underneath my skirt?'

'It's part of the oath.'

'But I haven't made a vow.'

'You don't have to here.'

'Elizabeth didn't tell me anything about this ritual.'

'Everyone who travelled through her did the same.'

Depression fell on my spirit. I left the forest, holding the edge of my skirt tight to my knees till I got home. I did not share this unsettling experience with my mother.

***

A couple of weeks later, I arrived in Moscow into the waiting arms of Elizabeth. She was a woman of about forty. She was tall and stout. I noticed that her head was very well placed on her shoulders. She looked elegant in her ankle-length dress, with a chain of diamonds round her neck. And diamond rings gleamed on her smooth fingers.

‘Are you Endurance?’

‘Yes ma.’

‘Welcome to *oyibo* land.’

Elizabeth lived in a three-roomed apartment with a huge sitting-room on the second floor of a large block of flats. The flat had a high ceiling. On one side of the living room, there were narrow stairs to a mezzanine. The rest of the living-room was furnished to make guests comfortable. The floor had a brown wall-to-wall rug carpet. There were four two-seater sofas, and coffee tables on the left- and right-hand sides of the sofas. On the coffee tables there were ashtrays, newspapers and magazines. And there was a well polished table on which a giant colour TV set sat. As I arrived, Elizabeth introduced me to two ladies (Abigail and Becky) who hugged and greeted me like a long-lost sister. Throughout that afternoon, the ladies were eager to hear news about home, and I did my best to bring them up-to-date.

The following morning, I helped them clean the flat. After breakfast, Elizabeth emerged from her bedroom in her pink dressing gown. She was chewing passionately on gum that kept her jaws firm and circling. She sat me down in the living room.

‘Endurance’, she said, ‘I spent $100,000 to bring you here. You’ll pay me all the money, and I want you to start work today. Some days, you’ll work at home here, and some days you’ll work outside. Is that clear?’

‘Ok ma. But $100,000 is a lot of money. How long will it take to refund it?’

‘It depends on you. Work hard! Now, give me your passport. You’ll have it back when you pay back my money.’

As we finished the conversation, Elizabeth got up her seat. She lit a cigarette, drew hard on it and exhaled huge smoke through her nostrils as she knitted her brows. She switched on the TV and played me a pornographic video. Initially I turned my face away.

'Look here,' she said. 'Our clients like this style. We offer them oral service as well. We charge different prices. Oral X: $80. X with condom: $100. And without condom: $150.'

I opened my mouth to speak, but I could not. An uneasy feeling caused a lump in my throat. Now I knew what I had been brought to Moscow to do.

That evening I had my first client. He was Fredrick, a young black man from London. He was tall and thin and his belly was slightly concave. He wore a skin-tight pullover, and his elegant bottom was outlined in skin-tight trousers. I saw in him a charm and some physical attractiveness. I imagined he was my boyfriend. He held my breasts, worked on my nipples with his tongue as he gradually moved his fingers deep down inside my body to stroke me. Before long, he laid me like a carpet and my legs were kicking jazz in the air. We had X for about thirty-five minutes without a condom. At the end of the service, Elizabeth said:

'How was it?'

'It's fine,' I said, as I was going to the bathroom to have a shower.

I saw a smile of satisfaction on her face.

When Fredrick came back again a few days later, he chose Abigail. I covered my face with my hands. I ran inside the room and wept. I felt like he had wrenched my heart out of my body and trampled on it. *Fredrick had cheated on me,* I thought. Just as he left, I realized that all the young man wanted was to have fun and that it was impossible for him to be faithful to me. And I had to separate my emotions from the profession. It was not about love, but about money. After Fredrick, I began to have regular X with white blokes, some of whom were as big as a hippopotamus.

One day, I lay down exhausted. I had done seven of what Abigail and Becky called 'full service'. Two of my clients must have taken powerful drugs to maintain prolonged erections as they pounded me for about forty minutes. I was still burning inside me when Elizabeth entered the room.

'No time to rest. You have two clients coming,' she said.

'Sorry. I can't take any more today,' I said.

'What! I won't have that,' she said, wagging a threatening finger at me.

From that moment Elizabeth assumed a hostile attitude. And I knew by the flush on her face that she was very vexed. But I did not take her finger-wagging seriously. *She was just testing my limit*, I thought.

Elizabeth left and five minutes later she came back to me. Her eyes flashed fire as she spoke.

'Now, get ready! A client will be here in fifteen minutes. Give him 'full service'. OK?'

'I can't. I'm still in pain, please.'

All of a sudden, Elizabeth moved closer like a tiger moving in for the kill. She slapped me hard across the face. I summoned my last strength and slapped her back. I ran to the kitchen; got hold of a meat knife; held it in the air, and threatened to kill her if she came near me.

'Wicked soul,' I said. 'Send me back home.'

'You'll pay me before I let you go. You've just called me a "wicked soul"?'

'Yes. I've my life to build and a poor mother to look after. My mother must not know I'm a prostitute here. Tell me! How quickly do you want to destroy my life?'

It tortured Elizabeth to hear me say that to her. She nearly did me grave bodily harm when the china teacup she threw sailed past my right ear and smashed against the wall. I still held on to my sharp knife waiting for her to come within an arm's length. Seeing the knife, she backed off and let me alone.

Two days later when tension seemed to have been defused, Elizabeth took me to a poorly lit area of the city. It was half past eight in the evening.

'Here's where you'll be working for now,' she said.

That night I saw many women walking the streets. Huge bums were exposed in their full horror in tight shorts and jean trousers. I watched the bums lurch by like hippos on the way to the water. That night I made friends with some Nigerian women. They told me stories about women who had been killed by mafia who, having had X with them, threw them out of fast-moving vehicles. They warned me to be very careful. One elderly woman among us that night told me she was desperately looking for a way to escape her ordeal. She regretted that it was not possible for her to go back to Lagos on foot. And as I was walking with her, she spotted an empty Pepsi can by the pavement and she took out her anger on it by kicking it further up the street. In the morning when I got back home, I locked myself up in my room, threw myself on the bed and wept.

A couple of years later, I was afflicted with a strange ailment which kept me off the streets.

One evening, I went to Elizabeth and said:

'For some time now, I've been experiencing acute pains in my stomach. And I've served you for three years and made you over $145,000. Give me my passport and set me free. Let me go and treat myself and start my own life. I beg you from the bottom of heart.'

'Who told you you've made such money?'

‘I keep a pocket notebook with me and mark a letter “l” in it for each client I’ve slept with. Now, they’re over five hundred.’

‘How much have you paid for your rent and feeding? I renewed your visa twice. It cost me money.’

‘But now that I’m sick, how long do you want to keep me for?’

‘I don’t care! You still owe $45,000 to me.’

As pains continued to claw at my heart and I was losing weight, Elizabeth began to see me as a loss to her business. She travelled back to Nigeria, apparently, to lure more women to Russia. In her absence, I managed to approach the Nigerian embassy. After hassling me with difficult questions about what brought me out of Nigeria to stain her image in Russia, they issued me with a Travel Certificate and bought me a ticket back to Nigeria.

As soon as I arrived in Benin City, I went to hospital for medical check-ups. The results of the medical examinations showed that I am HIV positive. Now, every day I take antiretroviral drugs (ARV) to contain the growth of the virus.

I am only twenty-one years old, waiting to die. But while I wait for my death to come, I see the need not to spread the disease but to join the campaign against prostitution and human trafficking. Now, I tell my tale to young women in schools, parents in marketplaces, and warn them to be wary of the likes of Elizabeth and Pastor Anozie who have ruined my life.

The Secret of a Lifetime

The DNA report I received in London that says I am not the biological father of my only child, Grace, acted on me like the blow of a whip across the face. My heart was in turmoil. I sniffed and blew my nose and wiped the tears now streaming down my face. It seemed a cruel and unjust fate had played a trick on me. I could have understood it if I had seen Grace's mother lead a wide life, play around with other men, or keep late hours. But she had done none of these things. Now she has taken the identity of Grace's biological father to the grave with her.

And Grace must not know this. But, how long can I keep the secret away from her? My new wife, Emilia, who also saw the report, is a chatter box. To keep Emilia's mouth shut is like trying to climb a wall leaning towards you.

I am Christopher Origogo. At the age of twenty-eight, after assessing the economic situation in my country, Nigeria, I strongly felt that the only way I could give my family a better life was by going to Europe to create economic prosperity. One afternoon I sat down with Grace's mother, Victoria, in the single room we lived together with our eight-year-old daughter in Lagos. I told Victoria about my burning desire to travel to Europe in search of a well-paid job that could improve my family's financial situation. And having listened to me, Victoria agreed that it was time to shake things up and she encouraged me to give it a go. She promised to look well after Grace in my absence.

I started to scrimp and save for the journey. Six months later, I paid a group of human traffickers who took me to Libya. I crossed the Mediterranean Sea on a rubber boat to Italy. When I saw the beauty of Sicily with its ancient temples and the neatly manicured hedges and lawns, my heart was racing and I could feel it pounding in my throat. The city reminded me of the European great cities that towered in magnificent splendor that I had read of and seen in my picture books in primary school many years ago.

'O God! If this is a dream, let it go on,' I said to myself.

But it was more than a dream. I could see and touch the objects around me. I was determined to work hard and overcome all odds in order for Grace and her mother to come to Europe.

Three months after my departure from Nigeria, I received a message from my mother saying that Victoria had lost her life in a car crash. I rocked my head in my hands, as a hard pain had started in the very middle of my forehead. For days I was beside myself with grief. And for weeks and months, I continued to see and talk to Victoria in my dreams. She would say to me:

'I'm with you. Stay strong and take care of Grace.'

When the news of Victoria's death reached me, I had crossed from Italy to Germany for a chance of getting a job. All the time I spent in Italy, I did not do a stroke of work, but it was not for lack of trying. Now with Victoria gone, I was plagued by worries about the welfare of Grace in custody of my ageing mother.

***

While in Germany, I settled down in a small town called Gosh to avoid the heavy police presence we often see in big cities because of my immigration status. The day I arrived in Gosh, I met an Ethiopian refugee, Hassan, who had lived in the town for five years. His manner was cheerful, and he was anxious to do whatever he could to help his fellow African. Hassan gave me temporary lodging. I told him I needed a job very badly for my survival and for the welfare of my daughter in Nigeria.

'Relax!' Hassan said, with a smile and unshakeable confidence.

A couple of days later, Hassan came home with a passport. The information in the passport suggested that it belonged to one 39-year-old black British citizen, John King. Hassan told me to memorize the name, place and date of birth and the nationality in the passport.

'In Europe,' Hassan said, 'you have to be smart and clever to survive.'

'But, Hassan, look at the age in the passport. I'm only twenty-eight.'

'Look! White man can't predict your age.'

I spent a whole day at home studying the information in the passport. Three days later, Hassan took me to Adecco to look for a job. We met a woman manager.

'Good morning! Are there any job vacancies?' Hassan said.

'For both of you?' the manager said, with a smile.

'No. For my friend,' Hassan said.

'Actually, we've got a vacancy in a chicken factory,' the manager said.

'Is it a full-time job?' Hassan said.

'Yes. Can I have your passport, please?' the manager said.

I fumbled in my pockets as if I was not sure where I had kept the passport. But the manager did not take any notice of the confusion, as she was now flipping through a fat file in front of her.

'Have it, please,' I said.

The manager inspected the passport. But, again, she failed to notice that the photograph in the passport did not bear any resemblance to me. She handed the passport back to me after she had made a photocopy of its information page.

'Sit down there and fill out this for me, please,' the manager said, as she handed me an application form.

When I came to the frames in the application form where the details of my bank account were required, I put down Hassan's bank detail, which the manager said was fine with her.

'Can you start work tomorrow morning?' the manager said.

'Even, now,' I said, quivering with excitement.

'We will pay your weekly wages every Friday.'

The manager gave me the company's address and the name of the supervisor I should see when I arrived. Immediately we finished with the manager and came out of her office, Hassan, with a good deal of satisfaction, gave his chest two resounding slaps. He hugged me and we hit high fives. I drew a deep sigh. *Could the spirit of Victoria be working for me?* I thought.

Two weeks after I started work, I rented a room, slightly bigger than a sentry box. It contained a sofa bed and a coffee table. I channelled my full energy into the job. I worked in the most difficult section of the production line. Before I started my twelve-hour shift in the morning, I would put on my overalls; a pair of wellington boots; and a pair of elbow-length rubber gloves. Then I would put on large plastic goggles and a surgery mask.

When chickens were brought into the factory from Belgium in long trucks in the morning, I would lift hundreds of live chickens by hand onto a long chain of slowly moving steel shackles. The shackles would then take the chickens (heads drooping, mouths drooling) to the blade where their throats were stabbed. At the end of my shift, all I could do was eat and fall like a log, shoes on feet, mouth agape.

Hassan did not disappoint. Every weekend he would come and give me my wages paid into his bank account, after taking his own five percent, based on our agreement. Every month, I sent my mother money for my daughter's wellbeing. I moved Grace from a state school to a fee-paying private school with more qualified teachers.

Two years later, I quit my job in the chicken factory on the advice of my thirty-two-year-old German girlfriend, Emilia. In the course of our courtship, I laid my life before her like an open book. I initiated her into my past life. I told her about my late wife, my little daughter in Nigeria and my immigration status in Germany. Emilia strongly warned that I could get myself into serious trouble with the police if it was discovered that I was working under a stolen identity. I returned my dodgy British passport to Hassan. With Emilia's help, I sought the services of her family lawyer who took my case up with the immigration officials. Emilia and I were later affianced.

Having lived in Germany for more than six years and got married to Emilia, I obtained German citizenship. Emilia and I relocated to the UK to widen a window of opportunity for me. I am more confident with the use of the English language than the German language. Emilia, on the other hand, speaks better English than I speak

German. Three months after we arrived in London, we were both employed by Marks and Spencer.

***

During my second annual vacation, I travelled to Nigeria to visit my family. The day I arrived in Lagos, I felt the sun warm on my back as I walked slowly along the road to the coach station to catch a bus to my birthplace. My shirt was beginning to stick to my back when I saw a bar a little way ahead. I decided a cold beer was just what I needed to slake my thirst. While I was drinking my beer, the memories of the time when I had hawked plantain chips in the streets of Lagos to eke out a living in the same harsh weather came flooding back.

Before long I took a bus and arrived in my town where my family was waiting to see me. I saw my mother first. She was sitting on a cane chair in front of the house, and was intent on peeling the potatoes on a tray she balanced on her knees. The noise from two big pieces of luggage I was hauling with me made my mother raise her head, and she let out a joyous shout immediately she saw me. It was as if a light had been switched on inside her.

'*Hey, ka bo ooo*!'

'Thank you, mama. It's good to see you.'

'Grace! Come, come, your father's here o.'

Grace jumped out. She hugged me tight. Her face was as bright as the sunshine.

'Daddy, daddy, welcome,' Grace said,

'I love you, my daughter.'

Instantly, I could see that the environment was not too good for Grace. There were some scaly rashes on her arms. I did not say anything about them so as not to kill the cheerful mood for my mother who was still on her knees, praising God for my return. Close neighbours joined my mother to welcome me home, while those not too close were at their front doors, smiling and looking happy for my mother. When my mother was back on her feet, she hugged me again.

'Christopher, my joy's full today. Many think you're no longer alive,' she said, raising her head skywards.

'Now, news will go round that I'm alive,' I said.

'Is Emilia ok?'

'She's fine, mum. She sends you a lot of greetings.'

Quickly, my mother left me and disappeared into the kitchen, and before long the delicious aroma of her cooking filled the area. After dinner, my family gathered together in the room my mother had made ready for me. I entertained them with stories and my experiences in Europe. I showed them the photos of my wife, Emilia. When they all left me alone to sleep, I could not sleep. The cruel singing of the mosquitoes in the room was too much for me to bear.

The following morning after breakfast, I bought a mosquito net which I rigged up over my bed. After a week, I had taken to my surroundings. One afternoon, I took a stroll with Grace to see the development the town had undergone since I left it. Here and there I saw beautiful and expensive modern houses with steep roofs and mullion windows surrounded by high fences. Grace told me they were built by local politicians. I noticed that while the politicians were creating the paradisiacal surroundings for themselves, there were a lot of people in the town, staggering under the burden of hunger, going about with sunken eyes and shallow cheeks. Some unemployed youths who had been rendered desperate by the absence of hope relied on internet scams for their income. I also observed that the poverty of my childhood days, which forced many families to hold up their hands in surrender to unhappy life, had not relaxed its squeeze.

One pathetic example was a case of a young girl, looking woebegone. She had no shoes on and was wearing a tattered T-shirt and a skirt, patched up several times at the back. She stood at the gate of one of the politicians' houses with arms outstretched in an appeal for alms. My eyes were blinded with unshed tears. I saw the image of my own daughter in the eyes of the poor girl. And I began to see the need more than ever before to arrange for Grace to join me in the UK.

I spent three weeks with my family. Before I came back to the UK, I obtained an international passport for Grace and I unlocked the mobile phone I brought home for her. The day I left I did not know that Grace had sorted out her things in a plastic bag with the aim to follow me to London. I was emotionally charged, battling to suppress the urge to cry, as I struggled to explain to her that she would need a visa.

'Daddy, please take me with you.'

'Grace, I'll arrange for a visa for you to join us in London within a month. I promise you.'

***

Two months after my return to the UK, I sent an invitation letter and other supporting documents to Grace so that she could apply for an EEA family permit at the British High Commission, Lagos. I gave the Commission my email address and telephone number as contact details. Fifteen days after the receipt of the visa application, the Commission sent me this message, addressed to Grace:

[...] As evidence of your relationship, you have submitted a certificate of registration of birth stating that Mr Christopher Origogo is your father. You have also submitted four photographs showing you and your sponsor together. However, these do not act as sufficient evidence to confirm anything other than that you have met. I therefore refuse your EEA family permit application because I am not satisfied that you meet all of the requirements of Regulation 7 of the immigration (European Economic Area) Regulations 2005.

The decision left me very disappointed. I phoned Grace to go back to the Commission and retrieve her passport and other documents. The Commission gave Grace a period of twenty-eight days within which to appeal against the refusal. I promptly appealed. I sent my daughter more documents: one hundred and forty receipts of Western Union money transfer, showing that I regularly sent money to my mother for the benefit of my daughter. My mother added Grace's mother's death certificate, and sixty family photographs, one of which showed Grace's mother standing beside me with my little Grace sitting at the back of my neck. The appeal letter with eighty pounds was sent to the 1-tier Immigration Tribunal in the United Kingdom. It took the Tribunal six months to send its reply to me. Again, it was addressed to Grace:

Dear Ms. Grace,
I write regarding your appeal which is being reviewed at post.
To enable us proceed we request that a DNA test is done to establish relationship between you and

your sponsor. The test should be arranged as soon as possible as we are unable to proceed until we get the results of the test.

The British High Commission sent me a list of eleven accredited DNA companies in the United Kingdom. I called all of them up. They all agreed to take Grace's DNA samples in Lagos and send them to the United Kingdom for analysis. As for my own samples, I was told to speak to my GP.

The cheapest price I could get for the DNA process was seven hundred pounds. I sat down on the carpet in my living room, thinking of how to get the money. Normally, the entry permit for an EU family member was free. I immediately approached my bank for an overdraft of two thousand pounds, in case of any other unforeseen expenses down the line. I was determined to pursue my daughter's case to the end. I paid one of the companies. Grace had her DNA samples taken at the British High Commission in Lagos, while I had my own taken by my doctor in London. According to the company, the analysis would take about three weeks to conclude, and the result would be sent to me and to the British High Commission. And three weeks later, this was the result I got:

Accredited DNA Paternity Test Report for case ref: DCX33000
Your samples have been analysed and our results are as follows:
Mother: NOT TESTED Swab No: N/A
Alleged father: Mr Christopher Origogo. Swab No: SW101611
Child – over 16: Grace Origogo. Swab No: SW101612

All of the above individuals donated consented cheek cell samples for analysis and had their identities warranted at the time of sampling by an independent Yd party. The improbability of paternity is 99.9997% based on the analysis of 15 independent DNA markers (using PowerPlex 16).
Hence the alleged father, Mr Christopher Origogo, cannot be included as the biological father of Grace Origogo.

My throat went dry as a biscuit. I felt a surge of helpless emotional torment that brought tears to my eyes. Grace's mother has taken the identity of Grace's biological father to the grave. And I have been permanently denied the chance to confront her with an inescapable request for a reason why I am just a foster father to Grace. I sat down in the sofa, thinking of what to tell Grace. I was unable to formulate a proper approach.

It now looked impossible that Grace would be issued a visa by the British High Commission in Nigeria. For two weeks I could not go to work. I entered a store and forgot what I wanted to buy. As soon as I recovered a bit from the trauma, I wrote to the British High Commission, explaining that the DNA result had done irreparable damage to my family. I also hinted about the long-lasting psychological effects it would have on Grace if she ever knew about it. I mentioned that part of any successful effort to keep the secret from her would hinge on having her with me in the UK. I appealed for her visa to be granted.

A couple of weeks later, I got an email in my inbox, asking Grace to submit her international passport to the Commission's office in Lagos. In the message, the Commission said that it took into consideration the fact that

I had been playing a paternal role for Grace, who might not have known any man other than me as her father.

When Grace arrived in London, the task of keeping her paternal status secret became a huge challenge. She lived with me and Emilia in a two-bedroom flat. I could not trust Emilia, even though she is kind and always keen to do whatever she can to please others. Emilia is a bit of a chatterbox. She can share issues of her own private life with strangers, as freely as she can share other people's affairs. The fact that I am not Grace's biological father was like a giant octopus spreading its tentacles all over me. And every time I looked at the innocent girl, beautifully made with legs long for her body and slim hips, my head was racked with pain. I felt I must cling to my self-control or I would go mad.

One evening after dinner, I called Emilia to the bedroom and raised the issue of Grace with her.

'Emilia, Emilia.'

'Yes, darling, you look worried. Why?'

'You know how sensitive the issue of Grace is.'

'I do.'

'In the family, it's only you and I who know that I'm not her biological father.'

'I know.'

'Think of the psychological effects on her if she knows about this.'

'I know.'

'The secret must be kept from Grace forever. Please, never, never, never, under any circumstances, talk about this with anybody. Not even with me anymore.'

'Darling, I understand everything. I promise never to think of this issue. Grace is your daughter, and she's my stepdaughter as far as I'm concerned.'

'Thank you, Emilia.'

In spite of Emilia's swearing to an absolute secrecy, I still felt that I had to do something to minimize any future risk of conflict between them. While I was still thinking of what to do, Emilia came to me in the bedroom one afternoon. I had just come back from work. She was working herself up into a temper. Her face was screwed up like a little baby's when it is just going to burst into tears.

'Come, come and see what Grace's done!'

My heart immediately began to pound inside my rib-cage, as I followed Emilia to the kitchen. Grace was in her room.

'Emilia, what's the problem?' I said.

'Your daughter dropped these two plates today,' she said, as she took out some pieces of broken plates out of the bin and showed them to me. 'Warn her! Next time she does this again I'll put her hot food on her palms.'

'Did you tell her off?'

'Yes, I did.'

What did Emilia say to Grace? And how did she say it? Nervously, I went to see Grace in her room to find out if she was in anyway hurt by whatever it was that Emilia had told her.

'Grace, you broke two plates today and Emilia was angry with you,' I said.

'I told her I was sorry,' Grace said.

'And what did she say to you?'

'She said if I broke more plates I'd eat my food from my palm.'

'Yes, she's right. So be more careful with the plates, OK.'

'OK daddy.'

'O, thank God! She called me "daddy,"' I said, as my heartbeat slowly returned to normal.

The following day after work, I ran to Sainsbury's to buy half dozen of plates to replace the broken ones. I thought the scene created by Emilia over ordinary broken plates was a warning shot.

But how long can this secret remain closely guarded? This is the mental agony by which I am being daily victimized.

The Mystery Pregnancy

This has nothing to do with me. But the situation is close enough to start me thinking.

Alice Hammer got herself into trouble when she was impregnated by the husband of her intimate and long-standing friend. She carried the pregnancy for thirteen months. One morning, as her painful experience worsened, she stared at her tear-smudged face in the mirror and wondered if she would ever smile again. She looked at her belly.

'Ah!' she said to it. 'It's because of you I'm going through this terrible ordeal.'

Alice was thirty-five, but she looked sixty with wrinkled skin like the neck of a turkey. She had once been happy. As a home economics teacher in a government college, she had been the dominant partner in her first marriage by which she had a four-year-old child, now in custody of its father. Alice had ended the relationship because she could not tolerate her husband being detained in the town beyond seven o'clock by political meetings. She had accused him of coming home late, swaying about like a tree in the breeze, with his breath contaminated by alcohol.

When Alice's marriage ended, she soon found a new love. It was Daniel Goddie, the husband of her friend, Janet.

***

Janet was a thirty-three-year-old Ghanaian, a fashion designer. She was a good example of a normal African lady, with high spirits and a great desire to enjoy herself. Janet had been married to Daniel, a successful Nigerian interior decorator, well known for painting houses and laying carpets in homes of well-to-do people in Benin City. The couple lived together in a well-furnished three-bedroom two-storey house with steep roofs and mullion windows. It was surrounded by a Viper Spike fence with an iron gate. Along the fence lines there were bushes of flourishing sweet-smelling flowers like Arabian jasmine. At the back of the house there was a leafy orange tree, under which Daniel and Janet usually sat down to play cards at weekends if the weather was fine. During working days, Daniel would join his wife at home in the afternoon, eat lunch and drink coffee. He would return for dinner at seven. Daniel and Janet had been married for four years without any children. Although there were no kids between them, the couple's relationship had remained steady and cordial.

One Friday afternoon, Daniel came home for lunch and met his wife playing Celine Dion's *I'm Alive.* Janet was in the living-room dancing, rotating her hips.

'Janet! Stop that music!' Daniel said.

'Danny, welcome,' Janet said, ignoring Daniel's order.

'I say, stop that music!'

Janet stopped the music abruptly. But she remained surprised at Daniel's aggressive behaviour towards her for no apparent reason.

'Danny today is my birthday. You've forgotten?'

'Why do you think it's worth celebrating?'

'I'm not throwing a party. I don't even invite my best friend, Alice Hammer. I'm only dancing.'

'You're happy, right?' Daniel said, ironically.

'Yes, of course! As you came in, I thought you'd come with my birthday gift. But your behaviour this afternoon is the unusual gift I wasn't expecting. Anyway, your lunch's ready.'

'Look, I've no appetite. I'm not happy looking at this house and no child is running around,' Daniel said.

'I know. I feel the pain more than –'

'You don't!' Daniel said, as he stormed out of the house without eating his lunch.

'Danny!'

Janet drew a deep breath. *Oh God*! Restless, she went to the back of the house and sat down under the tree, staring into space. That Friday afternoon, Janet was supposed to go shopping with Alice. She was supposed to buy fresh *tete* vegetables and goat meat in the market before it packed up at four. She just could not go out. Concern began to burn its way through her mind, as it slowly dawned on her that her relationship with Daniel was now in trouble.

When Daniel returned home, it was ten o'clock. Janet was at the door to welcome him. But Daniel swatted her hands away as she wanted to hold him and kiss him. Janet was not a woman to let the grass grow under her feet. She wanted to patch things up with her husband. As soon as Daniel changed into his pyjamas, Janet went to him.

'Danny, how was your day?'

'Fine'

'What can I make you? Now, you must be very hungry.'

'I'm not.'

'Then, can we talk?'

'It's too late.'

Janet went into her room. Her heart was thumping a painful beat. Throughout the night she tossed from side to side of her bed.

When Janet got up in the morning, her bleary eyes showed that she had not slept. She went to the kitchen, switched on the electric kettle and made Daniel his breakfast. She carried it on a tray over to him in his room.

'Morning, Danny. Here's your breakfast.'

'Leave it in the kitchen.'

'Danny! Why has it come to this? Please, be patient with me.'

'I can't. Your belly has been flat like a chopping board for four years? Let's end this whole thing.'

'What?'

'You heard me well.'

Janet's mouth dropped open, her eyes widened. She could not describe what a shock it was for her to hear Daniel say those words. She went into her room. She sat on the edge of the bed, and as her agitation grew she began to fidget with her wedding ring, turning it around and around on her finger as was her habit when nervous. She came out again.

'Please, don't destroy our relationship.'

'You'll need to go back home and rebuild your own life.'

'Remember!' Janet said, as unbidden tears began to well up in her eyes. 'I married you without my parents' consent. The disgrace will kill me if I go back to them now, saying you've kicked me out of your life.'

'That's your own business.'

Realizing that her relationship with her husband was in danger of collapse, Janet went to Alice to pour out her worries. When Janet arrived, Alice was sitting on a stool in front her house, removing pods of beans on a tray.

'Alice! I need your help and advice.'

'I hope there's no problem,' Alice said.

'Daniel wants to send me home.'

'Why?'

'I haven't given him a baby yet.'

'*No o o*! Why not talk to his family.'

'He won't listen to them.'

'Let's give him time to calm down. I'll try and talk to him.'

Two days later, Alice went to see Daniel in his office.

'Darling, Janet came to me to complain about you. I think she's getting the message. When is she moving out of your house?'

'Let's give her time to recover from the shock that we're parting ways. For three days she hasn't eaten anything, and she's been crying like an abandoned child in the midst of complete strangers. I'm scared.'

'I don't care!' Alice said.

But Daniel was trying to reduce tension between him and Janet. For about a month, the situation appeared to show some improvement, as Janet was trying hard to save her relationship with her husband. But, while she was trying to patch things up with Daniel, a strong rumour began to circulate that her husband was having an affair with Alice. She did not believe it, and she did not dismiss it either. She kept her eyes and ears open. Tortured by the fear of rekindling the flame of tension between her and Daniel, Janet did not immediately confront Daniel with the rumour. She asked herself: 'what good would there be in confronting my husband with information that I have neither power nor opportunity to turn to accuracy?'

One quiet evening Janet had made Daniel's favourite dinner and waited for him to return home from work. As Daniel entered the flat, the mouth-watering aroma of local *Jollof* rice and wild goat head cooked in garlic began to twitch his nostrils.

‘What’s going on here?’ Daniel said, as a smile flickered across his face.

‘Your dinner is ready, Danny.’

Daniel took off his timberland boots. He flung his tool box on the sofa in the living room, and sauntered to the dining room. Janet was there waiting to help him unzip his blue overalls. Daniel ate with mouthfuls, stuffing huge pieces of meat into his mouth. He washed the food down with a can of Coca-Cola. After the dinner, Daniel wiped his mouth with the back of his hand and praised Janet’s cooking.

‘Thank you, that was lovely.’

Janet quickly collected the dishes and put them into the kitchen sink while Daniel was still sitting at the dinner table removing particles of meat from between his teeth with a toothpick. Now Janet and Daniel sat facing each other.

‘How was your day at work?’ Janet said.

‘It was fine.’

‘Hmm, Danny, I need to talk to you,’ Janet said with an audible sigh.

‘About?’

‘I hear that you’re having an affair with my friend, Alice.’

Daniel went silent. The silence lasted about two minutes. He got up and strolled slowly about the living room and when he passed the windows, as though in idle curiosity, peeped through the curtains. Then, with his hands in his pockets, he returned to the dining room and sat on the edge of the table.

‘What’s your answer?’ Janet said.

‘Look, I’ve heard the rumour myself.’

‘And ...?’

‘It isn’t true.’

Daniel's denial was not satisfactory to Janet. A follow-up question sprang from Janet's lips, but she did not ask it. She asked another instead.

'Do you still love me, Danny?'

'I need a baby in this house.'

Choked with emotion, Janet left her seat and kissed her husband.

'I'll give you a baby boy.'

Janet was honestly attached to her husband, and was ever secretly hoping against hope to win back his heart. She asked Daniel to continue keeping his patience. And she wished she could have seen into Alice's mind to know its workings.

One afternoon, Alice visited Daniel in his office.

'Darling,' Alice said, with a big smile on her face.

'You're looking as beautiful as ever,' Daniel said.

Sitting on Daniel's lap, Alice said:

'I've good news for you.'

'What's it about?'

Alice fumbled in her handbag and brought out a letter and gave it to Daniel.

'Open it and read it, darling.'

As Daniel read the letter, the pupils of his eyes dilated.

'You're pregnant?'

'I'm at six weeks. My doctor confirmed it and asked me to come back at twelve weeks. You'll soon become a proud father.'

Daniel went wild with joy. He threw his arms around Alice, sprang close up, pressed his face to hers, and kissed her tenderly. For the first time in their secret affair, the miracle of love transfused them in a way that they were unconscious of time and place. They were not human any more, but two spirits united by a divine fire.

'I've been vindicated,' Daniel said. 'People think I'm a paper horse.'

'No. You can kick.'

'I have felt that I might be the only person in my family who will die without a child to inherit his fortune.'

'Blame that barren Janet. Now there's a good reason why she has to go. You've been too soft with her.'

Emboldened by the new development, Daniel saw an opening to force Janet out of his life. Daniel and Alice's affair was no longer a secret. Daniel started skipping lunch and dinner with Janet. He began to spend quality time with Alice. But Alice was not aware of the noose into which she was putting her neck.

Janet would have none of that. She went to Alice's school during lunch break. Alice sighted Janet first.

'Hi Janet, good to see you,' Alice said.

'So, you're behind my trouble with my husband?'

Alice swallowed hard. She felt a twinge of guilt and was unable to make further eye contacts with Janet.

'Ah! Who-who told you?' Alice said, stammering.

'Alice, leave my Danny alone. You fucking bitch!'

'*My friend*, it's too late. Go and sort yourself out with Daniel.'

Janet grew red in the face and her eyes bulged out of her head. She did really foam at the mouth.

'But I've come to warn you,' Janet said, wagging her finger at Alice, provocatively.

Alice tilted her head back and laughed like a hyena. She dismissed the warning.

'Don't come to me again. And for your information, I'm carrying Daniel's baby.'

Janet left Alice's school premises hurriedly. As she stepped into the road, an old Bedford truck that had seen better days almost ran her over. Her eyes were puffy.

She rushed back home to confront Daniel who was in the kitchen making a coffee for himself.

'Daniel!' Janet shouted. 'Your secret affair with Alice is exposed. She's even pregnant now. You can no longer deny it. Can you?'

'You're not the right woman for me. Go back to Ghana!'

'Let me remind you. When I married you, you had nothing. Now you're rich and popular. You think it's by your own efforts alone? Yes, I'll go. But you and that bitch will regret treating me this so badly.'

That afternoon, Daniel took some items of clothing and his wash-bag and left home.

Instantly, a look of cold hatred crossed Janet's face. She was poised to fight back. Janet knew she had a gift from God that enabled her to help people succeed and to destroy her enemies. When she was twelve years old, she was able to predict certain future events and dangers. She would read tarot cards for her schoolmates, and since her predictions usually came true, she became fascinated with the occult. She would follow her grandmother to *Ogboni* fraternity meetings. When she came of age, she was initiated into the group with the supernatural powers inherent in it. Now, she was fully ready to fight Alice with all her spiritual resources.

Janet went into her room and turned the key in the keyhole to firmly lock it. She brought out a folded red cloth underneath her wardrobe and unfurled it. She took out a small animal horn. In the cavity of the horn, there was sticky black soap into which a red feather was stuck. She held the horn like a microphone. She took out the red feather and licked the sticky soap around its nib. She stuck the feather back into the cavity of the horn. She began to swear viciously at Alice and Daniel.

A week later, Janet gathered up all her personal belongings and moved to Ghana.

***

With Janet gone, Alice moved in with Daniel. For Alice, it was a mission accomplished. But, when it was time for Alice to give birth to her baby, she could not. Nine months passed. Ten months passed. Eleven months passed. Twelve months passed. Alice was still unable to deliver her baby. As her situation had defied all medical solutions, Alice began to seek spiritual help. She turned to the church in search of miracles. She took part in several church services, some of which were organized like rock concerts, complete with hand clapping and fervent hymn singing. But her situation saw no improvement. The more the baby grew, distending her belly, the more the agonizing pain in Alice's body. And a lack of progress towards finding a solution had driven Daniel into a frenzy of frustration. He could not concentrate on his job, and he was falling on hard times.

Alice had become a laughing stock in her community. She moved out of Daniel's house to avoid the sneers of the locals. She rented a ramshackle mud house. The surface of its walls had been washed by many rains into the river nearby. Most of the houses in her neighbourhood had native roofs on top of them. The thatches on the rafters above some houses showed like a bone protruding through the skin. Some had windows without sashes and doorways without doors. Alice had decided that it was the only way to live and avoid the sneers and sniggers of those who knew her and her story.

One evening towards five o'clock, Alice went to the near-by river. She stood on the edge of the river, as a gentle breeze was fluttering the green leaves of the surrounding trees. The thought of suicide so as to escape from her seemingly intolerable bondage flashed through her mind. But it was interrupted by the melodious song of a singing bird which perched on a tree nearby.

Alice felt a sudden surge of emotion. She raised her head skywards, looked at the bird, and burst into a flood of tears. The bird took flight in fright.

'Lord! When will I sing my own sweet song?' Alice said to herself, as she was slowly walking back home, with a hand on her hip.

When she arrived home, Daniel was at the door with a shopping bag containing her dinner.

'Daniel, I'm dying.'

'Look, it's time to try a witch doctor.'

In the middle of the night, Alice remembered that she had once heard about a clever old seer, living alone in a small village half a mile away from her. Many people believed that the seer had powers other folks did not have in the whole of the region. But Alice was not sure if he was still alive. The following morning, Alice ate her breakfast hastily and set out to look for the man in spite of the bad weather condition of the day, as rain clouds were gathering. By the time Alice arrived at the seer's shrine, every layer of her clothes had been soaked. Alice knocked hard on the front door.

'Who you be?' A faint voice cut through the door from the within.

When the door was answered, Alice was facing a very old, tall and bent man, with bushy, fluffy white hair and a droopy moustache. He was wearing animal skin, sewn like a sleeveless padded jacket, on top of a raffia skirt. Seeing Alice with a big belly and her clothes completely soaked through, he said:

'Enter! Enter! *Wot* bring you here in this big rain?'

‘Papa, I need your help. I’m dying.’

‘Sit *don* here,’ the man said, as he slowly walked into one of the rooms in the house.

The man came out with a large blanket and gave it to Alice to keep her warm. He went back in. Alice felt enormous relief that the old seer was still alive. While the old man was still inside the room, Alice cast her eyes around the shrine to reassure herself that she was in the right place and with the right man.

The shrine was dimly lit with two kerosene lamps hung overhead, but it was bright enough for her to see that on one side of the walls, cheetah skin was used as decorations. There were bones, skulls and fresh bloody heads of certain creatures like cats and snakes hung on another wall. In one corner of the shrine, there was a big grinding stone with a small one on top of it for grinding medicinal leaves and grains. There were two rooms next to each other at one side of the shrine. One of the rooms was kept open and it looked like a pharmacy. There were shelves on the walls where dry and fresh herbs were kept in plastic bowls. There were also bottles of various shapes and forms, well arranged and labelled. Some bottles were empty. Some were half filled with liquids. One particularly interesting bottle was one which had a big belly and a long narrow neck. But inside the bottle, there was a single piece of chunky wood. It was a wonder beyond all telling how the wood made its way into the bottle.

Alice was still looking surprised when the old man came out. He sat down like a Buddhist, on the floor opposite Alice.

‘Youn’ woman, how I can help you?’

‘Papa, I’ve been carrying this pregnancy for twelve months now,’ Alice said, as tears trickled down her nose.

The seer did not ask Alice any further questions. Instead, he gave her cowry shells strung together like Catholic prayer beads. Following the seer's instructions, Alice rubbed the cowry shells against her palms, whispered her prayers and requests to them and handed them back to the seer. He then put some alligator pepper and two cloves of kola-nut into his mouth, chewed them together and spat the juice and the fragments of the substance onto the cowry shells in his hands. Then he threw the cowry shells onto a mat in front of him, and he began to chant incantations to consult with an ancient god. When the cowry shells landed on the mat, some faced up. Some faced down. And some sat on their edges.

Bad omen!

'Youn' woman, you have husband?'

'Yes papa.'

'Com' and see me with him tomorrow.'

'Papa, please what did the god say?' Alice said, looking ill-at-ease.

'He will talk again tomorrow.'

The following morning, Alice and Daniel went to see the seer. Alice's heart was pounding with anxiety. And the seer was there to receive them.

'Good morning papa. Here's my husband, Daniel.'

'Welcome, youn' man. Alice your first wife?' the seer said.

'No, Papa,' Daniel said.

'*Wer* the other woman now?'

'She left Nigeria twelve months ago.'

'Go and find her. Alice is under a juju.'

Daniel flung himself on the floor. He seized the seer's knees and implored him to find an alternative solution. What came by spell must go by spell.

‘Papa, please help us with your medicaments and counter-spell.’

‘Youn’ man, you think too much of my powers. I can’t break the spell. Medicine can’t cure it. Alice need forgiveness from the other woman.’

‘Papa, I won’t be able to find Janet.’

‘You must, for Alice to live!’

‘O, God! It’s finished,’ Alice said.

Alice’s disappointment expressed itself quite plainly like a nose on your face. Daniel rushed out of the shrine. He lit a cigarette, drew hard on it, blew a great cloud of smoke from his mouth and watched it fade into the air.

‘Now, you have to go to Ghana,’ Alice said.

‘I can’t go.’

‘Then do you want me to die like this, Daniel?’

‘But you understand that I can’t talk to Janet now about anything.’

‘You know her address, right?’

‘I can’t remember the number exactly. It’s either 12 or 14 Third Avenue, East Legon, Accra.

That night Daniel did little except smoke endless cigarettes and stare at the ceiling.

***

Two weeks later, it was Friday. The first pink and red streaks of dawn were staining the eastern sky when Alice put two items of clothing into a suitcase, took her handbag and travelled to Accra. She arrived late in the evening. She lodged in a cheap hotel near the coach station. The following morning, she washed her face and called a taxi from the hotel. She gave the address to the taxi driver. And when the taxi detached itself from the flow of traffic on the main road and entered Third Avenue, the driver announced:

'Madam, we're on Third Avenue. Watch for the number.'

Immediately, Alice's eyes began to work overtime, looking here and there, shifting from long view to short view, rejecting odd numbers and concentrating on even numbers.

'Wait, driver! That's number 12.'

The driver pulled off the road.

'How much do I owe you?'

The driver looked at his meter.

'Thirty-five cedis'

'I give you forty. Keep the change.'

Alighting from the taxi, Alice saw a shop with this sign at the top: '*Janet Mensa Fashion Design*'. Alice's heart was pounding in her rib-cage – *da dum, da dum*, as she was not sure how she would be received by Janet. As Alice entered the shop, she saw a woman sitting on a low stool, with a-month-old baby in the crook of her arm. She was holding the baby against her breast. Janet raised her head slightly to look at the visitor. Janet shrank into herself and drew back.

'Who's this?' Janet said, with a face twisted to a strange grimace.

'It's me,' Alice said, as guilt began to eat into her heart like acid.

'Why are you in Accra, and particularly here in my house?'

'This is the same pregnancy I've been carrying since you left Nigeria. I don't feel like I have a baby in my womb any more. And I'm ready to die in this way. Believe me! I've looked for death here and there. But, before I die, I must ask for your forgiveness for the wrong I've done you.'

Janet's recollection of her troubles in Nigeria flashed through her mind so rapidly that she could not hold any one image long enough on which to focus. She thought that, yes, Alice had received what she deserved but the thought did nothing to alleviate the painful memories that marred her relationship with Daniel.

'Please take a seat. Where's Daniel?'

'He's in Nigeria.'

'He wouldn't dare to come here and see me.'

'I know.'

'Alice, let me tell you I'm not responsible for your trouble. It's true that I was upset with you. But I've since moved on with my life. I'm now married to a gentleman here in Accra. And this is my baby. As a mother, I can only wish you an easy delivery.'

Alice left her seat, dropped on her knees, held Janet's feet, as tears trickled down her cheeks. She took out her handkerchief and dabbed them.

'Thank you so much.'

'What can I offer you?' Janet said.

'A can of Coca-Cola is enough.'

After long arrears of suffering, the night's vigil, and the insults of her humiliating condition had strung her to that point when pain was almost pleasure, Alice finally found relief. She went back to her hotel. She called Daniel to inform him that she had found Janet. Alice immediately went to bed and sank into a sound sleep. The right side of her face sank in the soft feather pillow, her cracked lips slightly parted as if she were trying to drink the pillow. The following morning, a little daylight that filtered into her hotel room through the window curtains woke her up. She went to the bathroom, brushed her teeth and had a shower. And after breakfast, she took her suitcase and headed to the coach station. Alice boarded a long distance bus back to Nigeria.

***

Back home, Alice, accompanied by Daniel, went back to the seer.

'Good afternoon, Papa! I'm back. I found the woman in Ghana. And I did what the god asked me to do,' Alice said.

'She forgive you?'

'I think so, Papa'

'Then, go home.'

One night, two weeks later, Alice began to experience some painful movement of the muscles of her womb. That experience became more intense the following morning. Alice called Daniel who rushed back from the office to give her the support she needed before heading to a birth centre. Daniel was running here and there like a hen with one chicken, trying to help Alice pack her bag, and holding her to steady her gait. After about eight hours of labour, Alice gave birth to a baby girl who had already grown two bottom teeth.

Too Broken To Mend

Every time I thought about the dramatic end to the dog-like devotion which Viola and I showed to each other in the course of our ten-year-old relationship, I still felt as if I were torn in half. My emotions would rise and fall. Even now, eight years since our separation, deep emotional pain occasionally strikes, and, often, without warning.

My graduation exam was only two weeks away. One night, Viola just lay in bed and talked and talked to me, nagging me all night long, asking me to arrange for an urgent holiday that would take us away from the UK. Even when I fell asleep and woke up in the morning, I could still hear her voice going on in the bathroom, threatening to end our ten-year-old relationship if no holiday was arranged within a week.

'Darling, why do you think this is the right time for me to go on holiday?' I said.

Viola did not respond. But her silence was punctuated by a gasping sob.

'Are you Ok?' I said.

'I hate you, Joe. I hate you!' she said.

I felt my blood freeze in my veins. It took me a good half an hour to persuade her to come out of the bathroom. When she came out, her eyes were red like an ember from a dying fire. I tried to hold her hand and explain that I was deeply worried about her threat to our long-standing relationship.

'Don't touch me!' she said, brushing my hand away.

Viola was a talker. Most times, she talked not because she had something to say but because she could not help herself. On the positive side, she was thrifty. This lifestyle was similar to mine.

Viola and I, having lived together for eight years as partners in Budapest, arrived in London to escape the economic hardship of the time in Hungary. On arriving in London, I got a job with Marks and Spencer as a customer advisor. Viola could not find a job because of her poor English. About a year later when her English improved, she got a job as a general assistant in Sainsbury's, where she chose to do only night shifts. Her monthly salary of over a thousand pounds was twice bigger than that of anyone in Hungary doing a similar job.

Now that both of us were employed, we agreed to continue to maintain the dog-like devotion which we had been showing to each other, and the symmetrical relationship that had supported our lifestyles over the years. We moved from a single room to a one-bed-room flat. We believed that it was time to try for a baby, and time to begin to save money to buy a house. We believed that in ten years, we could save enough money to buy a small house outside Budapest. A house, with a garden, nice pictures on the walls, nice carpets on the floors, where we could live and make merry with our families and friends.

Not long, in order to improve my educational status, I started studying part-time for a university degree while I worked full-time. And as for Viola, with no bias in expectation towards her, she enjoyed her time off work by going to solarium twice a week to tan her skin, and to the gym once a week to tone her physique. I know for a fact that Viola had a tremendous sympathy for the maintenance of her lovely figure.

Six months or so later, I had no recognizable evidence leading to the knowledge that Viola's attitude towards me would suddenly change. Now whenever she came back home from work in the morning, she would entertain me with stories of her colleague who had bought a new car or who had just arrived from their dream holiday. She began to question why I had not changed my job or become a manager in my workplace so that I could earn more money to buy a flashy car and money for regular holidays abroad. She set herself in opposition to anything I said or did to advance our collective interest. She even one day questioned why my ears were too far from my head.

This was the pattern of behaviour Viola was showing towards me on a regular basis. And the reason for it posed a formidable problem for explanation.

One morning she came to me after she had had her shower and said:

'I need one-week holiday.'

'Where do you want us to go to?' I said, reluctantly.

'We can go anywhere, but not within the UK.'

The fact that Viola wanted a holiday was not the issue, but requesting one when my graduation exam was two weeks away was what registered my shock.

'But our holiday will be perfect after my final exam,' I said.

'O yes! Stay with your exam. I can go alone, but if I do, I'm done with you.'

I trembled like a frightened child. Viola went straight to the kitchen and took her oral contraceptive which she had stopped using five months earlier.

'What are you doing? I think we're trying for our first baby,' I said.

'I don't need it anymore.'

'What's your trouble? Tell me!' I said.

'I'm no longer the right lady for you.'

She took off her diamond engagement ring, and flung it at me.

Later that morning, I went to work, but it was as if I had no business being there. I remember that I worked on tills on that day and there were three customers who complained that they had been given wrong change. After work, I rushed back home to browse the internet for the holiday. I was not prepared to let anything render asunder my ten-year-old relationship with Viola. To make a fresh start with another woman would be extremely difficult for me. Going through the internet, I found a nice place in Quarteira, Algarve, Portugal. I booked a room for two, for seven nights, at Zodiac Hotel, a short distance away from the sea.

'Darling, I've found a good place for us in Portugal.'

'O, you're feeling the heat,' she said, laughing.

'Go and get your luggage ready!'

Viola carried two heavy suitcases, which seemed too many to take with us on a short holiday. She took clothes enough to travel around the world.

'Why not just take a suitcase to carry our things in? We don't really need two for this trip.'

'Shush!'

***

We arrived at Zodiac Hotel in the afternoon. Viola put her hands in her trouser pockets while I struggled to get the suitcases out of the luggage compartment of the coach we travelled on from the airport. I hauled the suitcases to the customer service desk to check in. Our room was on the third floor. There was a sign on the door of the lift, saying that the lift was temporarily out of order. When I tried to ask a porter to help us carry the suitcases to our room, Viola said it was not necessary.

‘Then carry one suitcase. I’ll carry the other,’ I said, wiping sweat off my forehead with the sleeve of my shirt.

‘No, take the first one. I’ll wait here with the second. When you come back, you take it with us,’ she said.

I did not know whether to laugh or to be angry. There were the porters to turn to, bigger and more hulking than me. Indeed they had nothing to do but carry suitcases. And here was I, struggling unnecessarily with two ridiculously heavy suitcases.

‘Look, Viola! I’m not a camel. If backs were to be broken at all, better let the porters break theirs than break mine, since their lift is not working.’

So up went one suitcase on a porter’s back. It took him two trips to take all the suitcases up to our room. And when he had finished, he had no breath left to speak of. Our room was large. There were two single beds pulled together on one side of the room. Viola quickly pulled them apart. I did not say anything, or asked why.

Later in the evening, we went for a walk along the beachfront, and we took time to appreciate the beauty of the small town. The streets were impeccably clean. They were banked with trees, carrying sweet-smelling blooms the smell of which reminded me of a pineapple.

Every day for five days in Quarteira, we lay in the sun on the sandy beach from sunrise to sunset. Viola hardly talked to me. She always buried her head in one of the Hungarian versions of Agatha Christy’s novels. In the far corner of my mind, I could unravel that Viola had built a great wall of antagonism between us, and my relationship with her was now in great danger of collapse.

Before we departed Portugal, we took a day trip to the British side of Gibraltar, Spain, to see giant apes on the rock of Gibraltar.

***

Three days after we arrived back in London, one would expect that Viola would still be basking in the euphoria of our eventful holiday in Portugal. But that was not the case.

'It's now three days since we came back from Portugal, don't you think we should go to the disco?' she said.

'No problem. There's a nightclub, nearby in Wimbledon.'

'I don't like Wimbledon nightclub.'

'Where do you like to go to?'

'Soho'

'Why?'

'I want to meet celebrities.'

Now it was crystal clear that Viola was bent on ending the relationship, and it was no longer in my hand to save it. My sense of disbelief and anger had dissolved into resignation. I was calm in spirit and prepared for the ordeal ahead of me. Two weeks later, Viola said she had found a place and would like to move out. She demanded that I give her six hundred pounds, the half of the refundable deposit we put down for our rented flat.

'Where do you want me to get the money to pay you? We've just come back from holiday, and I haven't taken my next salary. You're leaving and you want to make me homeless?'

'I don't care!' she said, raising herself to her feet and charging to fury and flung at me one foul name after another.

Now, I strongly felt that I was at the limits of my endurance. Every effort I made to encourage Viola to reconcile her action with sanity was thrown back in my face. It was too late. I gave Viola three hundred pounds and my giant TV set which was worth three hundred and fifty pounds. And I wished her good luck.

***

Three weeks after her departure, Viola started calling my mobile phone. For two weeks, she kept disturbing my phone. I did not answer any of her calls. One evening, she turned up in my workplace with a mask of make-up on her shallow face. She looked so thin that it seemed as if her clothes were holding her together.

'Viola, please, what do you want from me again?'

'Please, Joe, give me the key to the flat. I'll wait for you at home. What do you like me to cook for you?'

When I arrived home after work, Viola had cooked fish soup waiting for me. But I was very afraid to eat it. I asked her again what brought her back to me. With a cry Viola flung herself down on my knees and begged for forgiveness. She begged me to take her back and put her out of her humiliating position. To her credit, Viola confessed to me that she had been two-timing me. She had been cheating on me with one of her male colleagues called Bernard. She said that all her nasty behaviour and ridiculous demands had been a ploy to frustrate me and cast me aside like a pair of worn-out shoes so that she could walk out of our ten-year-old relationship and join Bernard.

'The guy told me he was single. He told me a lot of things I wanted to hear. But, the fact is that he's living with his wife and two children in a council flat,' Viola said.

'Now, you want to come back to me because things did not pan out according to your plan.'

I thought Bernard had painted to Viola the life that a young woman could lead in a new relationship, and he had made it very alluring. After Viola's several days of emotional plea, I agreed that she should come back to me. Some people never appreciate what they've got until they lose it. Viola was such a person.

Viola came back home, but continually for three months she was crying; crying because her love for Bernard was still burning in her heart. It pained her that she had got it wrong with Bernard who was unable to return her love. And with me, it became plain like a nose on your face to her that I did not trust her anymore.

Unfortunately, Viola's return did nothing to put her out of her humiliating position. She sank into depression, left her job and moved back to Hungary.

A Bitter Taste

James Koko was thirty-five years old. He was a big man, both in stature and in heart. Apart from his size, he saw himself like a smart African youth with a desire to pursue a happy life with the tenacity of a bulldog.

James came to Hungary from Nairobi, Kenya, in July on a two-week tourist visa. He took a taxi from the airport to Astoria Hotel where he had booked a room to stay in for the duration of his visit. As a tourist, he had all the time in the world to do sightseeing. While visiting some historical places such as the Hungarian parliament and House of Horror, he observed that Budapest was a beautiful place. The roads were clean, and they were tarred up to the door mouths of houses, built together to form long lines on both sides of the road. And there were wide cement pavements on both sides of the road for pedestrians. He also noticed that there was no indiscriminate honking of horns by motorists. He sauntered to Blaha Lujza Square. He sat down in the park to watch people cracking cones of ice cream and soaking up the sun.

'Life seems pretty easy for this class of people,' he said.

James looked back at the situation in Nairobi where there were a lot of street hawkers, with hollow cheeks and sunken eyes, sidling through traffic jams to hawk plantain chips and oranges to eke out a living.

'I'll bring my children and Esther here to have this interesting experience.'

James had no intention of going back to his family anytime soon. A week before his visa expired, he began to look for the possibility of extending his visa, getting a job and accommodation. In one of his visits to Blaha Lujza Square, James met a Ghanaian student who had been living in Budapest for three years.

'Hi man, I'm James.'

'*My brother*, I'm David.'

The two Africans shook hands and hugged each other.

'David, I'm new here. Show me the way. I want a job.'

'Hmm, *my brother*, you're "*Jonny Just Come*"' (JJC), David said, laughing.

'This is not a laughing matter.'

'*My brother*, no jobs here. Even the citizens find work in other countries.'

'Then how do you survive?'

'If you're not a student getting regular support from home, go to refugee camp.'

'To do what?'

'Register yourself. You'll get free meals, and three extra months to live here legally.'

'But I need money to support myself and family in Kenya.'

'Ok, take my number. First, go to camp. I'll later give you a hint about how to make money without breaking a sweat.'

'David! Now you're talking.'

One sunny Sunday afternoon, James left his hotel and went to the nearest asylum centre known as Menekuteket Befogado Allomas in Bicske, a quiet town outside Budapest. When he arrived, the scent of flowers was wafted by the breeze into his nostrils. In front of the camp, there were flower beds that spelt the town's name in variety of colours. He was received by two porters who doubled as security personnel. James immediately found himself in a room with barred windows. It was virtually empty of furniture. No TV. The only article of furniture in the room was a rough wooden shelf with cheap editions of foreign magazines in battered shapes.

The following morning, the camp's social workers took James to an office where they played back a video concerning the camp rules, meal schedules, social and recreational activities. A few hours later, he was handed over to an immigration officer who took his details including his fingerprints and the photographs of his face.

'I'm Szabolcs,' the immigration officer said. 'I've been assigned to talk to you about your asylum application. Please, tell me your name, country of origin and your age for the record.'

'James Koko. I'm 35, Kenyan.'

'What part of Kenya are you from?'

'Nairobi.'

'Ok. What brought you to Hungary?'

'I fled because I converted to Christianity from Islam, and my family was after my life',

'How did you come to Hungary?'

'By air'

'Where's your passport?'

The immigration officer opened the passport and inspected it. After the interview, James was returned to the room which the refugees in the camp called 'quarantine.' James was required to stay in isolation until all necessary medical exams, including blood samples for human immunodeficiency virus (HIV), had been completed. James was already cracking up in isolation when he was 'de-quarantined' and transferred to the general dormitory which was more comfortable. Then he was issued with a quarterly renewable temporary resident permit which meant that he could move freely, but without the right to seek any paid employment until the final outcome of his asylum application.

James went back to David in Budapest for what he could do to get money "without breaking a sweat".

'You have your permit?'

'Yes.'

'*My brother*, are you man enough? You must be brave if you want quick money.'

'No worries. I'm a hustler.'

'Do you know *gbaana*?'

'No.'

'Then follow me! Open your eyes, and tell me what you see when we come back.'

David took James to a pub in the basement of a giant house where heavy gypsy music was thundering out. It was dimly lit with lights that turned every object to blue or purple. James saw that money was changing hands, but he did not see what the customers were paying for.

'Let's go out,' David said.

They came out and went into a nearby Macdonald's.

'What did you see?' David said.

'I saw that money was changing hands.'

'What else?'

'Nothing'

'Did you see people kissing each other?'

'O yes. I saw that as well.'

'That's the time the seller put the *gbaana*, wrapped in small pieces, into the mouth of the buyer.'

'Wow!'

'And when you see the *boys in blue*, you quickly swallow the stuff. In the morning you'll excrete them, clean them up, and try again. Fast money, you see.'

James went back to the camp and wrestled with his mind.

'Do cocaine? No. Prison is close by.'

When James' asylum application result came, it was unsuccessful. But he appealed against the decision. And while the outcome of his appeal was yet to be determined, James met a young Hungarian lady, Anita T, a nurse by profession. She was thirty years old. She spoke English patchily. After a brief introduction, James and Anita agreed to meet again. Anita would be happy to have someone to give her conversation lessons in English so that she might rub up her knowledge of the language.

After six months of platonic relationship, James invited Anita to the camp to visit him. Anita honoured the invitation. They strolled along a narrow pathway in the woods. The sun was shining through the trees, and the little woodland birds were twittering and flitting from bush to bush. As they were walking along James held Anita's hand in his and squeezed it gently. The twosome stopped. Looking at Anita with love-sick eyes, James threw his arms around Anita, sprang close up, pressed his face to hers, and gave her a passionate kiss. James' marrow melted in his bones like butter in the sun.

'Anita, I like you very much,' James said.

'You like Hungary?' Anita said.

'It's very beautiful. But the language is difficult.'

'I teach you *Magyar*. You teach me English. OK?'

'I like that.'

'Are you married, James?'

'No o.'

After a few more months, Anita and James' relationship became very close, and they agreed to get married. James left the refugee camp and moved to Anita's apartment in Budapest. Behind Anita's back, James would call his wife and talk to his two children in Nairobi. But when Anita and James got married, James stopped talking to his Kenyan wife. And when the

Kenyan wife, Esther, could not hear from her husband for a long time, she texted this message:

James, I'm deeply sad that you'd leave
Me here alone to raise your kids you've
Abandoned; come back; take up your role
As a father; I still love you with the whole
Of my heart; when you were in this area,
You were happy; you'll be again in Kenya.

James quickly deleted the message. And he warned Esther never to text him again.

After her wedding, Anita took her marriage certificate and James' passport to the immigration office. James was issued with a two-year family resident permit. He felt the wings of his spirit give a flutter of delight. *Thank God. Now things will begin to look up for me,* he thought.

But one chilly Monday morning, Anita and James were having a cuddle on the sofa in the flat. Two cups of steaming coffee were on a small table beside the sofa. Outside, the wind was blowing fitfully, driving rain against the window in savage bursts. As James was taking a sip of his coffee, there was a tap-tap tapping on the door. Koli, Anita's dog, sat up and began to bark. And Anita was startled into motion.

'*Ki az*?' Anita said, as she answered the door.

'Police.'

James was taken away to the immigration office. Anita accompanied him. While Anita sat down in the waiting room, an officer took James into a small room.

'My name is Lazlo,' the officer said, as he leaned back in his chair.

Lazlo took off his glasses and wiped them. They were very strong and hideously distorted his eyes. He flipped through a fat file in front of him.

'We received a letter through our embassy in Nairobi from one Esther Koko who claims to be your wife. She wants you back home. James, how many wives have you got?'

As James heard Esther's name, the saliva began to dry up in his mouth, and he felt as though his blood had dried up too in his veins.

'Wives!' James said. 'I-I have only one wife.'

'And who's that "only one"?'

'Anita, of course,'

'Alright, look at this photo. Is that you?'

Holding the photo, James' hand was shaking.

'No. This isn't me.'

'This is another photo, showing you, a woman and two beautiful kids.'

'Again, I-I don't know anybody in the photo.'

'James, you may not know that it's against our law to be married in this way.'

After the interview, James was kept in handcuffs and taken to another room, adjacent to the one in which he had been interviewed. Anita was called in. The language of conversation was entirely in Hungarian. But it is believed that the materials shown to James must have been shown to Anita, too, because at some point during the conversation, Anita burst into tears. And she kept uttering the words: '*Nem igasz*' (unbelievable). The moment James heard those words, be began to wrestle with his conscience. He had caused Anita a broken heart. Suddenly, James' own cry erupted from the room he was in.

'Please, let me see Anita, for a second,' he pleaded.

The police obliged him. James saw in Anita's eyes the grimace of a soul in pain. And with his hands handcuffed behind his back, James dropped on his knees.

'Anita, I'm so sorry. Forgive me.'

With her face puffy as if she had spent half the night crying her eyes out, Anita opened her mouth to speak, but found she could not.

Later in the afternoon, the police went back to Anita's flat to pick up James' international passport. He was driven to the deportation camp in Szombathely. While James was in the deportation camp, Anita went to court to ask for a divorce, and it was granted. James' stay permit was revoked. He spent several months in detention, gnashing teeth, before he was deported to Nairobi to pick up the pieces of his life.

The Giant Hydra

I have two scars on the left side of my belly. One is the size of a penny, and it is the entry point of a seven-inch knife that cut through my skin when I came under attack on foot patrol in the middle of the night. The other one is five inches long, and it is left by the surgeon's knife I underwent at Lagos University Teaching Hospital to deal with the damage done to my internal organs. This scar, with its sixteen stitches, now makes my belly look like a rugby ball.

My name is Joel Agbari. My interest in the Nigeria Police Force started when I was thirteen years old. First, in my primary school picture book, I often came across the picture of a policeman who bent double to help a gloomy-looking missing child. In the speech balloon over the head of the policeman in the picture book, there was this: 'Police is your friend'.

Second, the policeman at the time was resplendent in his uniform. He was dressed in a short-sleeve khaki shirt and shorts with knife-edge creases. He wore black high-shine Gibson shoes and knee-high woollen socks. When he donned his dark navy Scottish-style beret with a bobble or pom pom on top, he allowed it to fit well around his head, with the Nigeria police crest sitting vertically above his left brow. The only weapon he had was a baton. It was made of wood, and was typically twenty inches in length or little longer. It was fat at one end, tapered to afford a comfortable grip at the other. The end with the handhold typically had some turnings at the nether to prevent slippage.

Finally, the policeman at the time was highly respected. He was seen as the protector of life and property and the custodian of law and order.

***

I was seventeen years old when I was enlisted in the Nigeria Police Force. I was the youngest recruit in my squad in 1975. After my six-month training at the Police College, Ikeja, Lagos, I was posted to Itire Police Station near Surulere.

On my first night shift, I was on the roster to walk the beat after midnight. I took with me a baton, a three-battery touch-light, a pair of handcuffs and a pocket notebook. Scarcely had I started walking the beat when I encountered two young men who, I believed, had no business being on the streets at that ungodly hour. I stopped them.

'Hey, look at the time! It's 2 am. What are you doing on the streets?'

Quick as a flash, one of the men stabbed me in the belly and fled. Immediately, I started blowing my police whistle to call for help, and then gave hot chase, ignoring my life-threatening wound. Not long, some members of a vigilante group in the area joined the chase and arrested the criminal. These private citizens handcuffed him and bundled him into the boot of a car.

Now it was time to assess my wound. I was bleeding dreadfully and those around me had difficulty in staunching the blood. I saw that parts of my internal organs were already coming out. I was rushed to the police station and thence to Lagos University Teaching Hospital for treatment. After the operation on my stomach I was taken to the recovery room where I spent fifteen days. And when I was discharged, I stayed home for thirty days to allow for sufficient recovery time.

When I resumed duty, I was told that the accused whose name was 'Mohammed Ballah' had been charged to court with attempted murder. I was given the date the case would again come to court.

On the day of the court, I woke up at the crack of dawn and had my mind set at meeting my attacker face to face in court. I remember that I sat next to the police prosecutor who briefed me on the case.

And when it was half past nine, there were two hard knocks on the door of the Judge's chambers. The knocks came from within, ostensibly from the judge himself, heralding his entrance into the courtroom. My memory still retains some aspect of the judge. He was a big man in his fifties. He had a fat face, full lips, and a fleshy nose. He wore a black coat over a very high white collar shirt, a neat unobtrusive tie, and a pair of striped trousers. His belly hung in heavy folds under his shirt. *O ti je obe yo.*

'Call your first case', the judge said.

'Mohammed Ballah!' the court clerk called out.

Silence.

'The accused is absent, my Lord.'

'Is his surety in court?' the judge said, as he scanned his eyes round the courtroom.

'He's not in court, my Lord,' the court clerk said.

The judge issued a bench warrant for Ballah's arrest, and the case was adjourned for a month.

***

On the next adjournment day, I was in court in my uniform. The courtroom was packed. Those who did not have seats stood outside, looking in through the windows. I did not know why the courtroom was that crowded on that day. My case again was the first to be called by the court clerk. Neither the accused nor his surety was in court again on that day. The judge asked the clerk to choose a date for another adjournment.

While the clerk was flipping through his diary to find a date, I was possessed by fury. I stood up and showed the judge my wounds. Those sitting in front of me turned round to look at me, and I turned to show the wounds to those sitting behind me. The judge was stunned. His mouth dropped open, his eyes widened. And I noticed that the veins on his forehead stood out like knotted cords and I knew instantly that my boldness had irritated him. Amidst tears rolling down my cheeks, I said:

'My Lord, I'm only seventeen years old. As you can see, I'm still in the service of the nation. Where's the man who wanted to kill me?'

'Sit down young man before I lose my temper!' the judge said with a rasping voice.

I ignored his order.

'My Lord,' I continued, 'Look at the serious physical harm the accused inflicted on me. Where's he? I believe he was released on bail the same day he was brought before this Honourable Court, whereas I was still on a hospital bed fighting for my life. Now he's jumped bail.'

Now, the judge felt I was lowering down the prestige of the court. He gavelled me to order and threatened to issue a 'contempt of court' against me. That threat angered lots members of the audience. Loud angry voices rose behind me. When I turned to look, several people in the audience had stood up and were ready to cause trouble. They were shouting:

'This is wrong! This is wrong!'

Many of those standing outside the courtroom also felt a great deal of sympathy for me, as they began to rush inside to disturb the proceedings. The judge retired in panic to his chambers for his own safety. The suspects, who had been brought to court for trial, were hurriedly taken back by the police to the police van 'Black Maria' that brought them from detention facility. And all proceedings for that day were abruptly suspended. Many later complained that the judge was fond of giving frivolous bails and adjournments in order to frustrate or dissipate witnesses in cases in which he had shown personal interest.

I later learnt that the judge did indeed issue 'contempt' against me. But the police refused to carry out the order as it was deemed stupid. My Divisional Police Officer and the Commissioner of Police stood by me.

In spite of my disappointment in our Criminal Justice System, I still love the police and my country. Corruption is the one giant hydra.

I Love Edith

It was Pastor Mutombo who told me of her. Edith is completely blind. And instead of begging, she is giving.

One Sunday afternoon towards half past two the blue sky was cloudless and the air was balmy, and I was sitting sufficiently comfortably on a bench with my cold coke and cake in Blaha Lujza Square, Budapest, when I saw Edith passing by, using her white cane to scan her pathway for obstacles. I went up to her and told her I had heard about her and I would like to draw her into short conversation about her good work. She ran her fingers through her ginger hair. She shook it back and then let it spread over her shoulders in luxuriant curls. Her lips broke into a smile as she sat down with me. She was smart and cool and fresh in her stonewashed blue dungarees on a white T-shirt.

Edith is twenty-eight years old. She is a real beauty of a certain type. When she smiles she exposes pearl-white and small regular teeth. She has a tight little mouth, and an angelic face that burns itself into your memory, if you understand what I mean.

After a brief introduction, Edith ran her fingers on my face to know whether I was young or old, and whether I was wearing a moustache or beard. In the course of our conversation, she entertained me with the stories of the great things she had done with justifiable pride. She was as lively as a cricket. While she was talking to me, I kept my eyes fixed on her face, listening attentively. My heart cleaved to her as soon as we ended our conversation. From then on, we became friends.

Edith was not born blind. She did not lose her sight to failure of the cornea. She was born prematurely. To keep her alive, she was put in an incubator that kept her in hospital for six weeks.

'The professional blunder of the nurse who tended to me caused my blindness. I was given a massive overdose of oxygen,' Edith said.

In spite of her awkward predicament, Edith engages in humanitarian work. She is a successful practitioner of the art of helping the needy. She believes she can help alleviate the sorrow of others by means of kindness and thoughtful attention. She uses her white cane to scan her way to refugee camps across Hungary to help Africans with humanitarian relief, purchased with her disability allowance.

Edith loves African people. Her love stemmed from a lot of stories she has heard from TV about Africa, and from books she has read, using Braille.

'Some of these stories show that Africans are nice and that they live in open-minded society. The information makes me become very interested in African people, although I don't reject anybody,' she said.

Edith started humanitarian work three years ago. She joined a foundation for Africa, called Afrikáért Alapitvány in Budapest.

'The foundation has a school and it helps fund a hospital for poor African children in the Congo. The president of the foundation is Mutombo, a Congolese Pastor.'

Edith is a devout Christian and an enthusiastic student of the Bible. At the age of 12, she decided to be a missionary. Every night, she faithfully performs the midnight prayers.

'I have a daily contact with God whose words have been my inspiration. Every day I invite Jesus Christ into my life. He leads me. He shows me whom to help, who should be my friend, and whom I should run away from,' she explained.

As part of her humanitarian work, Edith travels across the country to counsel the refugees and teach them Hungarian language. And she sometimes leads them to community centres to introduce them to the locals. One morning, Edith ignored a dark gusty wind, heavy with the smells of the thawing, sour earth, that was tossing the clouds about and cutting through the body like a blade of ice. She had heard that some refugees were about to be deported to their countries. And she saw it as part of her humanitarian work to see the refugees through their difficult days in the deportation camp. She headed for Szombathely. When she met some of those to be deported, they were badly shaken by the unpleasant reality of having to be returned home to become destitute. She offered them prayer, advice, and lovely scented flowers and a basket of provisions.

'Not only giving gifts to those to be deported, but I also talk to refugees who live here on how they can properly integrate. I take them along with me to visit Hungarian communities so that they can have friends among them. I also engage in practising Hungarian language with some of them. In this way they can blend with the society,' Edith said.

Edith cited a case of two Africans who were in the deportation camp in Szombathely. They had accused the police of keeping them in jail for months without due process. They said they were not allowed access to legal aid.

'It's unfortunate that I couldn't secure their release. But I took it upon myself to visit them and give them moral and material support. It's not only the refugees this time. There was a small girl from Romania in orphans' asylum who became dejected because she seriously felt that her life had lost meaning. She threatened to stop going to school. But when I met her, I talked her out of doing so. So she finished secondary school. And today, I hear that the same lady is attending a college.'

While many in the same condition as Edith are downcast, or are suffering from low self-esteem, Edith shows a lively sense of pleasure in and satisfaction with every bit of what she does to help the less-privileged foreigners in her country.

Edith said: 'I know that I have a lot of disadvantages because of my condition. For example, it's difficult for me to find information. I can't browse the internet for information, and I can't read every newspaper or magazine. It may be true that some others in the same condition as me are downcast. I'm not. As I said earlier, God is my strength, and I derive my joy from his support. I enjoy the fact that my heart is not polluted by what eyes can see. A lot of people judge the others by their looks, and then often form negative opinions.'

As Edith travels around the country for her good work, there is no doubt that her trips cost a lot of money. But how does this young handicapped lady get financial help? She never stands on the street corner with a hand outstretched in an appeal to the compassion of the passers-by for alms. She said she bore the costs of whatever she did to assist people with her disability allowance.

'But I must add that my friends and the refugees themselves have been very supportive of my effort. They always encourage me. I hear their love for me in their voices. I don't like begging. But if somebody gives me a gift, I'll appreciate it and be thankful. But I won't ask them,' Edith said.

We dream sweet dreams. The dream of this young born-again Christian is to make a tour of Africa and evangelise, and ask the Africans about their views of life.

'Because of this desire,' Edith said, 'I've begun to learn handicraft which I'd like to teach the Africans who can later make money out of what they learn from me to improve their lives. The money from the handicraft could be used to help some poor villages, or be used to buy medicines for the sick.'

Printed in Great Britain
by Amazon

46439333R00067